Friend or Foe

CHAPTER 1

HIS MOTHER WOKE HIM AS USUAL THAT morning, shaking his shoulder and then kissing him gently as he rolled over. It was pitch black around him, but then he was used to that by now. For months they had slept down in the cellar on the bunks his father had made the last time he was home on leave.

'Here's your apple, dear,' his mother said. 'Sit up and have your apple now.' And she patted the pillow behind him as he pushed himself up on so his elbows. He felt the saucer come into his hand. His early morning apple was the only thing that had not changed since the war started. Every morning as far back as he could remember his mother has woken him this way – with an apple peeled, cored and quartered lying opened up on a white saucer.

He felt his mother shifting off the bed and watched for the flare of yellow light as she struck the match for the oil lamp. The cellar walls flickered and then settled in the new light, and the boy saw his mother was dressed to go out. She had her coat on and her hat with the brown feather at the back. It was only then that he remembered. His stomach turned over inside him and tears choked at his throat. The morning he had thought would never come, had come. Every night since he'd first heard about it, he prayed it might not happen to him; and the night before, he had prayed he would die in his sleep rather than wake up and have to go.

'You were restless again last night, dear. Did you sleep?' He nodded, not trusting himself to speak. 'Come on now. Eat your apple and get dressed. Quick as you can, dear. It's six o'clock by the station, they said. It's a quarter-to now. I left you as long as I could.'

Fifteen minutes left. Fifteen minutes and he'd be gone. Thirty minutes and she would be back in this house without him. She was bending over him, shaking his shoulder. 'Please, dear. We must hurry.

Eat it down, quickly now. Miss Roberts said you'd be having a roll and jam on the train, but you must have something before you go.'

'Don't want it, Mum.' He handed the saucer back to her. Only moments before he had been savouring that first bite of his apple. They were always crisp, always juicy, like nothing else. But now he felt sick at the sight of it.

'You must, David. You always have your apple. You know you do.'

He had upset her and ate it to make her happy, swallowing it like medicine, trying not to taste it. Each bite reminded him that this was the last apple.

Once out of bed he dressed to keep the cold out. His mother was packing his suitcase and he watched everything going in and wondered where he'd be when he took it all out again.

'They said only one case, so there's only room for one change of clothes. All the things you wanted, they're at the bottom. I'll send on the rest as soon as I know where you'll be.' She smoothed down his coat collar and brushed through his hair with her fingers. 'You'll do,' she said, smiling softly.

'Do I have to, Mum? Do I have to go?' Even as he asked he knew it was useless. Everyone was going from school – no one was staying behind. He was ashamed of himself now. He'd promised himself he'd be brave when he said goodbye. He clung to his mother, pressing his face into her coat, fighting his tears.

She crouched down in front of him, holding him by the shoulders. 'You remember what I said, David, when I told you your father had been killed? Do you?' David nodded. 'I said you'd have to be the man in the house, remember?' He took the handkerchief she was offering. 'You never saw your father crying, did you?'

'No, Mum.'

'Men don't cry, see? Try to be a man, David, like your father was, eh?' She chucked him under the chin, and straightened the cap on to the front of his head. 'Come on now. We'll be late.'

It was still dark up in the street, and a fine drizzle sprayed their faces as they walked away from the house. David looked back over his shoulder as they came to the postbox at the corner and caught a last glimpse of the front steps. He felt his mother's hand on his elbow, and then they were round the corner.

Ahead of them there was a glow of fire in the sky. 'South of the river,' his mother said. 'Battersea, I

should say. Poor devils. At least you'll be away from all that, David, away from the bombs, away from the war. At least they won't get you as well.' He was surprised by the grim tone in her voice.

'Where will you go, Mum?'

'Wherever they send me. Probably to the coast – Kent or somewhere like that. Somewhere where there's anti-aircraft guns, that's all I know. Don't worry, I'll write.'

Their footsteps sounded hollow in the empty street. They had to step off the pavement to pick their way round the edge of a pile of rubble that was still scattered halfway across the street. That was where the Perkins family had lived. They had been bombed out only a week before; they were all killed. Special prayers were said at school assembly for Brian and Garry Perkins, but no one ever mentioned them after that. They were dead, after all.

In the gloom outside Highbury and Islington Underground Station there was already a crowd of people. Miss Evers' voice rang out above the hubbub and the crying. She was calling out names. His mother pulled at his hand and they ran the last few yards.

'Tony Tucker. Tony Tucker.' Miss Evers' voice rose

to a shriek. 'Where's Tucky. Has anyone seen Tucky?'

'He's coming, miss. I saw him.'

'And what about David Carey? Is he here yet?'

'Yes, miss. I'm here, miss.' David spoke out, pleased at the strength in his voice.

'Here's Tucky, miss. He's just coming.'

'Right then.' Miss Evers folded her piece of paper. 'We're all here, and it's time to go. Say goodbye as quick as ever you can. The train leaves Paddington at half past eight, and we have to be there at least an hour before. So hurry it up now – and don't forget your gas masks.'

David felt the case being handed to him. 'Goodbye, David. And don't worry. It'll be all right. I'll send a letter as soon as I can. God bless.' She kissed him quickly on the cheek and turned away. He watched her until she disappeared at the end of the street. All around him there was crying: boys he'd never dreamt could cry, weeping openly, and mothers holding on to each other as they walked away. He was glad his mother hadn't cried, and it helped him to see so many of his friends as miserable as he felt himself. He blinked back the tears that had gathered in his eyes and wiped his face before turning towards the station.

The warmth of the Underground came up to meet

them as the school trooped down the silent, unmoving escalator. They followed Miss Evers along the tunnels, down the stairways and out on to the platform. Tucky came up alongside David and dropped his suitcase.

'H'lo, Davey.'

'H'lo, Tucky.' They were old friends and there was nothing more to be said.

They did not have long to wait. There was a distant rumble and then a rush of warm, oily wind that blew their eyes closed as it rushed into the platform. Miss Evers counted them as they pushed and jostled into the carriage, herding them in like sheep, so that every corner of the carriage was filled. The doors clicked and hissed shut, and the train jerked forward, throwing everyone against each other.

David watched the last Highbury and Islington sign as long as he could, craning his neck until the carriage plunged into the darkness of the tunnel and it was gone.

'That's that, then,' said Tucky next to him. David nodded and looked up at the parallel rows of handles that swung from the roof of the carriage, always out of reach. And he remembered his father lifting him up high above everyone, and how he'd hung on to the strap next to his father's looking down on a sea of upturned faces.

Miss Evers was shouting at them again. 'Boys, boys. Can you all hear me, boys? Sam, you're not listening. I can see you're not listening. You can't listen and talk at the same time – it's not possible. Now, we've been through all this many times before, but I'll do it just once more to make sure. We're going to … where are we going, Tucky?'

'Devon, miss.'

'What station do we have to go to, to get to Devon, Tucky?'

'Don't know, miss.'

'Paddington, Tucky. We're going to Paddington Station.' Whenever Miss Evers wanted to tell them all something, she always asked Tucky first; and when Tucky didn't know, and he never did know, that was her excuse to tell them herself. She picked on Tucky mercilessly, and David hated her for it.

'And what am I going to give you at Paddington Station, Tucky? Can you remember that, Tucky?'

'No, miss.'

'Your placards, Tucky. With your name and address on. Remember? In case you get lost.'

'And the string, miss,' someone else said. Tucky was already sniffing, his hands screwed into his eyes. Another question from Miss Evers and he would dissolve into floods of tears.

'Well, I'm glad someone was paying attention. Placards and string. You'll be wearing the placards round your neck. Remember now, Tucky?' Tucky nodded into his raincoat sleeve, and Miss Evers left him alone after that.

They had to change trains once and Sam left his case behind on the train. Miss Evers screamed at the guard and the doors hissed open again and she went back in for it. When she came out she screamed at Sam, but Sam braved it out and then grinned sheepishly as soon as her back was turned.

Placards strung round their necks, and two by two, the boys climbed the long stairs up into Paddington Station. David and Tucky were almost last in the crocodile and as far away from Miss Evers as possible.

Up to that moment it had been just his school that was being evacuated, but now David discovered that every other child in London seemed to be at the station. Miss Ever shouted back at them to hold onto the belt of the boy in front and they wound their way like a long snake through the crowds of milling children and screaming teachers, who paused only to blow their whistles. And above it all came the thunder and rhythmic pounding of steam engines, and the rich, exciting smell of the smoke.

David had been on a train once before. Just before the war started he'd been on a school journey to Birchington, but then his mother and father had been on the platform waving him off. He felt the belt in his hand jerk and the crocodile stuttered forward again towards the platform.

Miss Roberts, the headmistress, was waiting for them by the ticket barrier; and so was Miss Hardy. Miss Roberts was in her usual bird's nest hat, and Miss Hardy, as usual, was clucking around her like a worried hen. Miss Evers seemed relieved to see them, and smiled for the first time that morning. Miss Roberts took charge and beckoned everyone closer.

'The train's at least two hours late, boys, so we'll have to wait. Put your cases down and sit on them.' It was good to have Miss Roberts there in her hat and bright clothes. There wasn't a boy in the school who didn't like her, and now her smiles and laughter were familiar and comforting in the strangeness and noise of the station.

David spent the two hours chatting to Tucky and looking at everyone else – that was all there was to do. The marches blared out of the loudspeakers, but they were so loud he could hardly make out the tune – and when there was a tune he recognised, a great explosion of steam would ruin it for him. Miss Hardy gave everyone a roll and jam with a mug of warm milk, and Miss Roberts sat heavily on her suitcase and smoked her way through a packet of cigarettes.

It seemed as if the train would never leave, but it did – three hours late. The boys piled into the train, fourteen to a carriage, and the train stood there, hissing gently.

David and Tucky found themselves sitting in Miss Roberts' carriage. They knew it would mean cigarette smoke all the way to Devon, but that was better than Miss Hardy's fussing, and a lot better than Miss Evers' waspish tongue. Miss Roberts collected all their placards and put them in the luggage rack above their heads.

'You won't need those for a bit. I think I know who you all are.' Miss Roberts sat down next to Tucky, and the seat sank. 'You'll need them again when we get to Devon – if we ever do.' She took off her bird's nest hat with a flourish and shook out her red hair, and then settled down to a packet of Senior Service cigarettes and a pile of orange paperbacks.

She was a huge lady, and Tucky wondered if he would ever be able to stop himself from sliding down towards her into the crater she had made in the cushioned seat.

Doors were banging all the way down the train and a group of sailors ran past waving and shouting.

More banging, the shrill whistle, the pressure building up in short blasts of steam; and then the train heaved forward, the engine settling into a slow pulling rhythm as they watched the platform slip away.

'We're off,' said Tucky.

'On our way, boys,' said Miss Roberts. 'Say goodbye to London, and good luck. Not for ever, you know. We'll be back.'

David stared out of the window and wondered what his mother was doing at that moment and how long it would be before he'd see her again.

CHAPTER 2

IT RAINED ALL THE WAY FROM LONDON TO Exeter. Miss Roberts hardly lifted her head from her books, unless it was to pull out another packet of cigarettes from her handbag. David and Tucky played noughts and crosses until they ran out of paper, and they were left staring at the window waiting for the next stop.

David passed the time by tracing drops of rain as they ran in intricate and erratic patterns from the top of the windowpane down towards the bottom. He would find two or three droplets that began life at the same time at the top, and watch them race each other to the bottom; and sometimes they would join together and plummet down in a great flood.

They stopped frequently and that did help to

break the monotony of the journey; and lunch of a sandwich and a biscuit at Westbury was a chance to stretch their legs and to empty the carriage of Miss Roberts' cigarette smoke.

But lunch was Tucky's downfall. He began to go white almost as soon as the train pulled out of Westbury, and a few minutes later was as sick as a dog. Miss Roberts did her best, but there were no corridors on the train, so all she could do was to hold his head, while the rest of them tried to keep as far away as possible. It was all cleared up at the next stop, but the after-smell still hung on, and Tucky's face was still a pale shade of green. He looked dreadful, and David tried to ignore him and to concentrate on the line of the hills in the distance. He thought it looked like the pictures of Devon he'd been shown at school, but they were still hours away from Exeter, and as the journey dragged on, his thoughts returned again to his house in Islington.

Tucky was feeling better. 'My mum said it won't be long,' he said suddenly. David said nothing. 'She said the war would be over in a few months and we'd all be home again. So it won't be long, will it?'

'Depends on who wins it.' David said.

'We'll win it,' Paul Browning said from the other

side of the carriage. 'Everyone says we'll win it.'

'Then it'll be a long war.'

'Who says?' Paul was sneering.

'That's what my dad said,' David replied quietly. He hated mentioning his father, and he hadn't meant to. He felt vulnerable now. 'He said that if the Germans win it'll be a short war and if we win it'll be long.'

'But we won last time,' Tucky piped up. 'We won then, didn't we?'

'Yeah. He's right,' Paul was learning forward. 'We won all right, and what you can do once, you can do again. That's right, isn't it, miss?'

'What is, Paul?' Miss Roberts looked up.

'The war, miss. Davey says we won't win it. You heard him, miss. We beat them last time, so we will again. Stands to reason, doesn't it miss?'

Miss Roberts closed her book. 'No, Paul. It doesn't stand to reason.' She sounded firm, and everyone listened when she sounded firm. 'I think we shall win in the end, I certainly hope we do. But it will not be in a few weeks or a few months. It may take a long long time to win – a year, two or three years, who knows? You must understand that you will not be going home for some time. You'll have a new home and a new school and it won't be easy for you. But it will be a lot easier if you can understand that you won't be going home for a long time. One day we'll all go back to Islington, but not for a long time. Understand?'

It could not have been clearer. David had won his duel with Paul, but it gave him no pleasure. He would gladly have lost one little argument for some ray of hope from Miss Roberts. There was none. The carriage fell silent and remained that way until the train pulled into Exeter Station. It was dark already and they were hungry.

Placards were put on, cases checked, then they were on the platform, and out into the cold. Tucky and David stuck together while Miss Roberts gathered the whole school around her for a roll call. Then she led the way through the ticket barrier and towards a waiting bus. There were people everywhere, but it was not like the bustle and noise at Paddington. Here they were standing and staring solemnly as the boys straggled through the ticket hall.

'Where you boys from, my dear?' The ticket collector put his hand on David's shoulder and turned him round.

'London,' said David.

'I know that, my dear,' he laughed easily. 'I know that right enough. But whereabouts in London.'

David felt foolish, and flushed. 'Islington,' said Tucky.

'Not heard of that, have you?' He asked around him and everyone shook their head. 'Off you go then, my dear, and keep smiling.' David did not know what he should be smiling about, and he could not help wondering how anyone could have reached the age of that ancient ticket collector without ever having heard of Islington.

'Talk funny, don't they?' said Tucky, as they rushed after the others.

Miss Roberts marshalled them into the dark green coach in the station yard, and David sat with Tucky on the long bench seat at the back and waited. They all waited, but nothing happened. Then someone realised the driver was missing, and a policeman went off in the dark to look for him. The boys sat numbed in their seats, every one of them exhausted, too exhausted even to be homesick. The driver came back eventually, and there were angry words in front of the bus – Miss Evers was giving him a piece of her mind.

The blackout was in force, and the headlights of

the bus were hooded so that only a thin slit of light struck the road ahead. The engine throbbed underneath them and the bus moved at last.

The journey through the dark lanes seemed unending. David sensed they must be out in the countryside because there were no houses. All he could see were high hedges and the occasional glimpse of a field as the headlights skimmed over it through a gateway. No one spoke in the bus. It was too noisy, but no one felt like it anyway. Tucky had gone to sleep on David's shoulder, but kept waking up every few minutes to ask if they were there. Halfway down the coach David could make out the shape of Miss Roberts' hat as it was lit up from time to time by the glow of her cigarette.

'This is it,' the driver's voice shouted, and the coach slowed down. Tucky woke up with a start. 'Round this bend and you're here.'

'Placards and cases,' said Miss Roberts. 'Don't leave anything behind.'

'And don't forget your cases, children,' Miss Hardy echoed. 'Make sure it's your own case and no one else's. Check them now, children.'

The bus had stopped, but David could see nothing out of the windows. He rubbed an island clear of steam and peered through. They were in a small square surrounded by low buildings. A door was thrown open in the darkness and a shaft of yellow light flooded out towards the coach.

'Everyone out.' Miss Roberts walked sideways down the centre of the coach. 'And mind your manners now.'

The lights of the village hall were blinding at first and David blinked and squinted his way down the hall. There were faces all around him, peering red faces and eyes that followed him. He looked away and followed on up some wooden steps and on to a platform. There were two long benches and David found himself in the back row and Tucky slid in next to him. It was warm in the hall and from somewhere came the smell of tomato soup, red tomato soup.

It was thick and not too hot, and they were each given a great hunk of brown bread which they dunked into the white enamel cups. David ate his slowly, savouring the warmth. Every new mouthful sent comforting shivers down his body. He had hoped for some of Tucky's but clearly Tucky was feeling well enough now to finish his. Then there were cheese rolls, and they washed it all down with the sweetest cocoa David had ever tasted. The cocoa was too much for Tucky and he emptied his into David's mug, and David crouched over it warming his hands.

Down in the hall everyone had stopped talking and Miss Roberts was speaking. 'The boys have all had a very long day, and I think we should get them off to bed as quickly as we can. But I know they'd all like me to thank you kind people for our welcoming meal. It's a long time since we've eaten like that. Now most of you are having one boy to stay and some two or three. Do choose quickly. They're a good bunch of boys, and I know you'll look after them as well as you can. You'll find their names and ages on their placards, so as soon as you've chosen the one you're having, please register with Miss Evers at the table by the door. That way we'll know where everyone has gone to. It wouldn't do to lose anyone now, would it? Take the first row first and then the back row will move forward.'

The crowd of faces in the hall moved in closer, looking up at them. The children sat sipping their cocoa and gazed back down at them. There was a lot of whispering and it was a long time before anyone moved. Then one of the ladies stepped forward and peered closely for a moment at Paul's placard. She smiled up at him over her glasses.

'Come on then, Paul,' she said, tapping him on the knee. 'Let's get the ball rolling. You come along with me.'

'Yes, miss,' said Paul and looked to Miss Roberts for reassurance. Miss Roberts nodded.

'Off you go then, Paul. And be good now.' Miss Roberts spoke kindly, and Paul got up and walked down the steps into the hall. The lady took his case and the two of them walked away towards Miss Evers' table at the back of the hall.

'Doesn't know what she's in for,' Tucky whispered from behind his cocoa mug. And David smiled for the first time that day. He sipped his cocoa and looked around the hall, trying to pick out a face he liked, but there were too many people and they were too remote to be real.

It was a smooth enough business after that. One by one the chairs on the platform emptied and soon the whole front row was gone. Miss Roberts beckoned the back row into their places.

Sam went. Billy Preston and Graham Watts went together, and gradually the hall was emptying. There was a small knot by the registration table, and Miss Roberts was with them. There was something wrong, David could tell that. Everyone kept glancing back up at the platform where David and Tucky sat side by side at the end of the front row. There was no one left.

'I'm sorry, Miss Roberts,' one of the ladies was saying. 'I'm sorry, but there's been an upset.'

'They have to sleep somewhere, don't they?' Miss Roberts sounded crisp. They were speaking in that urgent half-whisper that adults use when they don't want to alarm listening children.

' 'Tis Mr Reynolds out to Hamleigh Farm. He's not come in to collect. They were all told. Half past eight he was told, like the rest. 'Tis past eleven now. Can't think where he's to.'

'But even with Mr Reynolds, that still leaves one boy unaccounted for,' Miss Roberts insisted.

'That'll be all right, you'll see, my dear. We'll find him somewhere. Poor little scrap.'

Tucky leaned closer to David. 'Davey. If they can't find anyone to look after us, will they send us home, d'you think?'

'Doubt it.'

'But what will they do with us then?'

'Miss Roberts will see us right,' David said hopefully. 'Don't worry, she'll see to it.'

'Davey. Why do you think no one chose us?' Tucky droned on in his flat voice.

'They didn't choose me, 'cos you were sitting next to me, and they didn't choose you because I was sitting next to you. And besides, we're not the prettiest in the class, are we?' He tried to joke it away, but he was hurt inside just as Tucky was. Time and time again people had looked him over and passed him by. 'Anyway,' he went on, 'I didn't much like the look of them.'

'Nor me,' said Tucky. 'Nor me.'

The arguing at the other end of the hall had

dwindled to an inaudible whisper now as they all realised the two boys might overhear them. But the longer it went on, the more obvious it became that the situation was serious. No one else seemed to have room for an evacuee, and it looked very much as if Mr Reynolds might not be coming at all. Finally Miss Roberts suggested they should give the boys a bed in the hall for the night, and someone went off to look for mattresses and blankets. Miss Hardy looked as if she would burst into tears at any minute, and Miss Evers kept throwing up her hands in digust. Meanwhile David and Tucky sat alone up on the platform, too tired and bewildered even to care what happened to them.

They had pulled away the chairs to make room for the newly arrived mattresses and bedding when the hall door banged open. A huge, bearded man in a great woolly coat and knee-high gaiters strode into the hall followed by a rangy-looking black and white sheepdog. Everyone gawped.

'I'm sorry to be late, but I've come for a boy.'

'You are Mr Reynolds I presume.' Miss Evers' voice was stiff with anger.

'I am, my dear, and who may you be?'

'Mr Reynolds, these children have been up for

over fifteen hours now.' Miss Roberts took Miss Evers' arm to stop her, but Miss Evers would go on. 'They have travelled nearly three hundred miles. You keep them waiting for another two hours or more and all you can say is you're sorry.'

Mr Reynolds looked down at Miss Evers. 'Lady, I've said I'm sorry. There's nothing more I can say if that won't satisfy you.' Then he looked up at the platform and walked towards the two boys who had stood up by this time. The dog followed and sat down by Mr Reynolds' feet, looking up at them.

'Sorry to keep you,' he said, looking from one to the other. He had bright blue eyes and the lines on his face disappeared into a beard that was flecked with white at the chin. There was wet mud down the front of his coat and David noticed a broad gold wedding ring on his hand as he ruffled the dog's neck. ' 'Twas the mare that did it. She foaled just half an hour ago, and I couldn't leave her. She had a bit of trouble, always does, this one. But we managed between us, and 'tis a good-looking foal, another colt though. Five foals she's had, and not a filly among them.'

'Filly?' said Tucky. 'What's that?'

'Horse, my dear,' and Mr Reynolds face creased

into a smile. 'Filly's a girl horse. Colt's a boy, like yourself.'

'Mr Reynolds,' one of the village ladies came up beside him. 'Mr Reynolds, which one will you have?'

'Which one?'

'You put yourself down for one, Mr Reynolds. You said you only had room for one.'

'You want me to choose between these two boys, is that it?'

No one replied. He looked from David to Tucky and back again to David. ' 'Tis just like market day,' he said, shaking his head.

'Mr Reynolds!' Miss Evers stamped her foot in fury.

'This one's the fatter,' Mr Reynolds went on, looking at Tucky, 'but then this one's taller.' He reached out and gripped David's arm. 'He's a bit skinny, you know, not much meat on him.'

'Mr Reynolds, this is a serious matter,' said Miss Evers.

'You're right, lady, no doubt about it. 'Tis a serious matter. I'm supposed to look at two young lads, face to face mind you, and then pick out one and not the other. Right enough, that's serious. 'Tis revolting that's what 'tis. And what happens to the one I don't choose, eh? How d'you think he'll feel?'

'As a matter of fact,' said Miss Roberts quickly, 'we don't know what will happen to him.'

'You don't know!'

'Apparently there's been a mistake, a muddle over numbers, and one of these two boys has nowhere to go, not yet anyway. I don't suppose you'd consider taking them both on, would you? They're great friends at school, and we'd be very obliged.'

'Friends, are they?' Mr Reynolds considered the two boys carefully and read each of their placards slowly, stroking his dog all the time. 'I'll tell you one thing for certain, it'll be both of them or neither. There'll be no choosing. What about asking them? They might not like the look of me – have you thought of that?' No one said anything, so he asked them direct. 'Well? What d'you think? I'm a farmer, forty-two years old, married, no children. My name's Jerry Reynolds, I run ninety-six acres – barley, sheep, milking cows, a few beef cattle and since the war began a few acres of potatoes. 'Tis only a small cottage, and you'll have to share one bed and do your bit about the farm. Well? What d'you say?'

Tucky looked at David and David looked back at him. It was the first good moment of the day – each understood instinctively what the other wanted.

'We'll go with you, mister,' David said.

'Mr Reynolds, my dear, that's what you'll call me. And I'll be glad to have you both. Now take those things off around your necks and get down here. You've given me a crick in my neck talking up at you like this.'

'Thank you, Mr Reynolds,' said Miss Roberts, shaking him by the hand. 'I've been their headmistress up till now, and they'll do you proud. You won't regret it.'

'I hope not,' Mr Reynolds said. 'Come on then you two, we'll be off. Haven't had my dinner yet. First the lambing then that confounded mare – quite put me out, it has.' The dog followed them towards the door.

'Mr Reynolds,' it was Miss Evers again. 'You must register before you take them.'

'Register?'

'It's regulations,' said Miss Evers icily. 'We have to know where the children are.'

'But you know that already, my dear,' Mr Reynolds smiled down at her. 'They'll be staying with us at Hamleigh Farm. Now you put that in your register, my dear. Goodnight to you.' Anyone who put Miss Evers in her place was all right with David and Tucky.

It was cold outside and drizzling, and the boys pulled their coats around their legs inside the van and huddled together on the front seat. The van smelt like an animal, and as Mr Reynolds banged the door and got in beside them, they heard a rustle behind them. David twisted round in his seat and peered into the darkness.

'One of my orphan lambs,' said Mr Reynolds. 'Mother died this morning and I can't persuade any of the other ewes to take him on. He keeps warm in the back there – plenty of straw.'

'That dog,' said Tucky. 'Where's that dog?'

'Jip? He never comes in the car, doesn't trust it. He'll follow along behind – he always does.' The van started up with a rattle and a roar. 'Comfortable?'

'Yes thanks, mister,' said Tucky.

' 'Tis Mister Reynolds, Tucky. Can you remember that?'

CHAPTER 3

THE LAST LEG OF THEIR JOURNEY WAS BUMPY, noisy, smelly and draughty, but for David and Tucky it was the only enjoyable part of a long day. Now they were no longer going away, they were arriving. Every jolting minute was bringing them closer to a new home. They sat forward in their seat anxious for the first glimpse of the cottage, and then the thin beam of the headlights caught the glint of black windows ahead, and the car bumped off the road down a rough track and stopped.

Mr Reynolds clicked open the latch on the front door and had to bend his head as he went in. It was a long, low kitchen with a stove at one end and an oil lamp burning low on a table. It smelt of cooking and oil fumes. Mr Reynolds picked up the lamp and led them up a narrow, winding stairway.

'I told you you'd have to be in together,' he said turning up the lamp. Shadows lightened and the room grew bigger. 'But there's good in everything. You'll be warmer this way. Your wash basin's on the chest, and there's a lavatory just outside the back door – through the kitchen. Don't forget to turn out the light before you go to sleep, will you?' He ruffled Tucky's hair and smiled broadly. 'You'll be all right then, my dears?'

'Mister ... Mister Reynolds,' David corrected himself quickly. 'You said you were married, where's ...?'

'In bed, my dear. Ann's in bed. We get up with the light here and try to go to bed when it's dark – same way as the animals. You'll be seeing her in the morning.' He turned to go.

'G'night,' said Tucky.

'Good night to you both, and never you worry. Us'll be all right together.' The door closed.

David tried the water in the wash bowl with the tip of his finger, but that was all the washing he did. Tucky didn't even bother to do that. He had his pyjamas on in a flash and was in bed before David had started to undress.

Once in bed the two of them lay staring up at the bumpy ceiling.

'Wonder what's happening to the others,' said David.

'S'pose we'll be like brothers, you and me, kind of anyway.'

'Something like,' David muttered, wishing he'd kept his socks on like Tucky.

'I like that Mr Reynolds,' said Tucky and he pulled the quilt up tighter to his chin to shut out the cold air.

'Wonder what she's like, Mrs Reynolds; Ann he called her, didn't he?'

'Be all right if she's anything like him,' Tucky said.

'What, beard an' all?'

'Get off, didn't mean that,' Tucky giggled. 'Turn that lamp down, like he said. Here, listen. You can't hear anything, and you can't see anything. Can you hear anything Davey? Davey? ... David?' But David was asleep, and before he had time to worry about it, so was Tucky.

In the morning it was the smell that woke them, and they dressed as if the house were on fire. They opened the kitchen door quietly. There was the sizzle and smell of frying eggs, and the thick gluey bubble of simmering porridge. Mrs Reynolds was bent over the kitchen stove with her back to them. She was small and slim and her dark hair was done up in a bun. The boys waited for her to turn and see them, neither of them wanting to make the first move. They stood transfixed by the smell until Mrs Reynolds turned with the saucepan of porridge in her hand.

'Morning, Mrs. I'm David and he's Tucky.' David came further into the room. Mrs Reynolds' eyes widened in shock and they saw the porridge saucepan jolt in her hand. She looked from one to the other, and then put the saucepan down slowly. 'You frightened me for a moment. I thought you would still be in bed. I was going to call you when Jerry came in.' There was something different about her voice, and David noticed it immediately. Yesterday he had become used to the sing-song burr of the villagers. That was difficult enough to understand at times, and they did have some funny ways of putting things, but this was the halting accent of a foreigner. 'Of course, Jerry has told me about you. He said you looked like ghosts, no red in the face. And he was right too. A good hot breakfast and a day outside in the country air – that would be good for you, no? I am Ann, you must call me Ann, and you are David and Lucky.'

'Tucky,' said Tucky. 'It's Tucky. Tony Tucker, but everyone calls me Tucky.'

'Good. So you are Tucky and you are David. I'm right?' The boys nodded. 'Now, come and sit down at the table. Jerry will be in soon. He has to milk cows and feed the animals all before breakfast, you know.'

Breakfast lived up to expectations, and Ann fussed over them until they could eat no more. Just as they finished, Mr Reynolds came in.

'Feel better then, my dears? There's not a better cook in all England than my Ann. No doubt about that, no doubt at all.'

'My mum's good,' said Tucky.

'Course she is,' Mr Reynolds was pulling off his boots by the door. 'I forgot that. Let's say my Ann is the best cook in all Devon, and that with your mother Tucky and David's mother here the champion cooks of London, there's not a cook in the kingdom to touch them. Agreed?'

'Agreed,' said David, anxious to repair any offence Tucky might have caused. Tucky always said what he felt, and David was used to it by now.

Ann bustled over to Mr Reynolds now, prattling on happily in her strange accent. Everything about her was small, and next to Mr Reynolds she seemed even smaller and more delicate than she was. There was a gentleness in her eyes that was immediately comforting to David and Tucky; and whenever she smiled, and that was often, her whole face seemed to shine.

Tucky studied Mr Reynolds as he devoured his breakfast. 'Can I see that baby horse?' he asked suddenly.

'Baby horse! Baby horse!' Mr Reynolds roared with laughter. 'Did you hear the boy, Ann? I told you, my dear, 'tis a foal, not a baby horse. A baby's a small one of us. Never make the mistake of thinking animals are like us. There's names for animals and names for us so that we can tell the difference. Animals are animals. You and me, Ann and Davey here – we're people, and that's different.'

'Baby horse or foal, Jerry,' Ann said, 'I think Tucky wants that he should see him.'

'And so he shall, Ann my dear, so shall they both, but after I've finished my breakfast – if they can wait that long.'

For David and Tucky it was worth waiting for. All that day and the next they saw things they'd never seen before as Mr Reynolds shepherded them around the farm. They watched him helping the foal born the night before, pulling him up on to wobbly legs. They discovered that the sheep on the steeply sloping fields were not wild after all; and the three milking cows, golden brown and white patches, wandered slowly towards them and did not attack. They watched Mr Reynolds delivering the early spring lambs, and helped him bring in the ewes that would be lambing soon. Then there were stakes to be driven in for fencing, water to be carried to the troughs in the fields and yards to be cleared. The two boys went everywhere with him, and Jip, the rangy black and white sheepdog, trailed along behind them.

By Sunday night David and Tucky knew their way

round the farm and felt as if they'd been there for months. They felt at home. Neither of them had given Islington or home a thought. They had been too busy for that.

In bed that night the boys lay in the darkness, whispering.

'Which do you like best?' said Tucky.

'Can't say,' David whispered back after a long pause.

'I wish my dad was like him,' Tucky went on. 'I've never heard him shout, not like my dad. My dad's always on at me.'

'My father never shouted, not often anyway,' David tried to picture him shouting and couldn't.

'Can you remember your dad still?'

'Course I can. He was only killed a year ago. Year ago last month. Course I can remember him.'

'Bet you hate them after what they done to your dad. I would.'

'Course I do, everyone hates them.' And David tried to imagine his father's plane crashing on the beaches, as he'd done so many times before.

'I think she hates them too,' Tucky whispered.

'Who? Ann?'

'I asked her if Mr Reynolds was going to go away

and fight, and she said he wouldn't be going. He's got to work the farm, and anyway he fought in the last war, wounded an' all. Then she asked me about my dad and I told her and she asked all about you and your dad, so I told her. She went white as a sheet, honest she did. Didn't say anything, but she hates them, I can tell.'

'You shouldn't have told them. That's private, just between us,' said David.

'But she asked, Davey. I had to tell her, didn't I? Couldn't lie, could I?'

'School tomorrow,' David muttered. 'Be funny, all of us together in a different school, with different teachers. Wonder how all the others settled in. Wonder what the teachers will be like.'

'Can't be worse than Miss Evers,' said Tucky, and he tugged the quilt farther over his side. 'You keep pulling it over your side. I was frozen this morning when I woke up.' And David tugged it back and buried himself further down the bed.

Ann sent them off early the next morning for the walk to school. 'Not far short of three miles,' Mr Reynolds had said. 'You'll do it inside three parts of an hour, no question.' It seemed more like ten miles.

Every bend brought another one and every hill a steeper one ahead. Jip came along with them, as far as the crossroads at the end of the lane, and then he stood looking after them, his tail drooping mournfully.

They ran the last half mile down into the village, their gas masks banging up and down on their backs. They had seen the village from the Reynolds' cottage. It stood on a hillside, a cluster of cottages with thatched roofs grouped under a tall grey church tower.

The village came upon them suddenly. They ran round a bend by a sign-post, and there was the school, just as Ann had explained. It was a long, low, gabled building built of purple-grey stone and grey tiles mottled with lichen. The playground outside was full – they were not late. Once inside the gate, they looked around for their friends from Islington and tried to ignore the inquisitive looks and huddled whispers of the village children.

'Where are they all?' said Tucky.

'P'raps they're late.' But the bell went as David was speaking.

The school was one big room on the one floor with a great black boiler at one end, and two long rows of desks, the row at the back on a raised floor so that the children could all see the blackboard in front. There were only twenty or thirty children there, boys and girls.

Coats were hung up by the door and gas masks over the backs of the desks, and everyone sat down – everyone, that is, except David and Tucky, who stood bemused by the door clutching their lunch boxes and gas masks.

At the far end of the room, beyond the boiler, a door opened, and there was a sudden and immediate silence as an old man walked slowly and deliberately towards the teacher's desk by the blackboard. As he sat down, all the children stood up and chanted in unison, 'Good morning, Mr Cooper'.

'Sit down,' the teacher said quietly. 'Good morning, children. The roll call please, Angela.'

'They got girls,' Tucky whispered. 'Do you think this is the right school?'

'Did you say something, lad?' The old man had swivelled round in his chair and was looking at them over the rims of his glasses.

'We were wondering, sir,' David said. 'We were told to come to school here, but none of our friends are here, so we thought perhaps we were in the wrong school.'

'You're David Carey and Tony Tucker?' They nodded. 'Then you're in the right place. In this school we always call the roll first before we do anything else. Do you understand?' He spoke clearly and kindly.

Angela called the roll, and each child stood up in turn, and then last of all she called out 'Tony Tucker', 'David Carey'. Mr Cooper then stood up and shook both of them by the hand.

'Welcome to our little school. I am the one and only teacher and my name is Mr Cooper, though no doubt the children call me something else. I require you to be polite, honest and hard-working. That is all. I hope you'll be very happy whilst you're with us.'

'What about all the others?' Tucky asked.

'Your friends from London have all gone to Imberleigh school. It's bigger there and there's more room.'

Mr Cooper turned to speak to the class. 'David and Tucky are evacuees, children. I told you we might be seeing new faces soon, didn't I? Well, here they are. I want you to remember that they are away from home, and that we are all very strange to them. We must all look after them and make them feel at home.'

Their welcome from the village children was cautious enough at first. But in morning playtime they were crowded into a corner under a big elm tree and bombarded with questions about London, about their homes, about German bombers. For a few days they felt they were the centre of attention. Whenever either of them spoke up in class everyone listened, and they were invited to eat their packed lunches at every house in the village. But it soon wore off, and within a few weeks they had been accepted as two 'townies' who were part of the village school.

There was a new pattern to their lives, broken only by letters from mothers, and the occasional glimpse of Miss Roberts in her hat whenever she came to the village. David's mother was stationed on an ack-ack battery on the south coast and wrote once a month. Tucky's parents were still in London but hardly ever wrote.

There was the walk to school after breakfast, usually in the rain; then morning prayers and the first lesson always with the gas masks on, when they all sat sweating and trying to concentrate on Mr Cooper's voice. Unless the sun was shining they took their packed lunches to a friend's house where there was always warm cocoa. After afternoon lessons there was the long walk home to the farm. Jip would meet them at the end of the lane by the crossroads, and they would race him home to tea with Ann in the smoky warmth of the kitchen. All that spring there were long walks on the moor that came down to where the farm ended. Mr Reynolds kept some sheep up there and the two boys came to know it well.

The war, London and Islington seemed to be in another world. Of course David looked forward to his mother's letter and kept every one under his pillow, and read and reread them whenever he could, but they seemed unreal.

There were signs a war was on. Mr Reynolds went off on Home Guard duty twice a week; there was a searchlight and an observation post in the village, and of course they still had their gas-mask drill. But there were no more bombs, and there was no more fear. They came to recognise Churchill's gruff voice over Mr Reynolds' crackling wireless set, and they noticed that Ann lost all laughter in her eyes whenever the war was mentioned. But it hardly ever was. Mr Reynolds used to say he was too busy to worry about the war.

Then one night in June the skyline of the moor

was lit up with gun flashes, and a distant crump of bombing miles away on the other side of the moor brought the war back to David and Tucky and shattered their new-found peace.

CHAPTER 4

DAVID AND TUCKY WATCHED FROM THEIR bedroom window. The single beam of the searchlight from the village circled the sky above them, hesitating and retracing as it patterned the darkness.

They were alone in the house that night. Mr Reynolds had been called out on Home Guard duty, and Ann went up the village with him to warm up the soup for them. It happened like that once a week and the boys were left to look after things on the farm.

'Like firework night,' said Tucky, resting his chin on his hands. And it was. There was the orange glow of fires, and the tracer for the anti-aircraft guns peppered the horizon with flashes and trails of hyphenated lights. They watched it as if it were a display. It was all a long way away, very different from the London raids they had both been through. Here someone else was being bombed, not them.

'Tucky!' David whispered, grabbing his arm.

'What?'

'Listen! Can't you hear it?'

It was clear enough now, the deep throb of aircraft engines, punctuated by spluttering. They leaned farther out of the window and craned upwards, scanning the night sky. It came from over the moor, and they saw it at the same time, a red flicker first, and then three more lights floating down through the

sky above the moor. But the throbbing and coughing had stopped now, and there was silence.

'The searchlight,' said David. 'Why doesn't it come this way? They'll miss it.'

But the searchlight was carving up the sky above the village at that moment, and the boys followed the lights as they fell lower and lower until they disappeared behind the moor.

'It's gone,' said Tucky. 'It's a German, wasn't it, Davey?'

'Crashed, must've crashed. It was going down all the time.'

'There'd have been a bang, an explosion or something.' Tucky pulled his head back inside.

'Could have landed,' David was thinking of the flat valleys on the moor. 'Could have, you know. There's places where a plane could land out there.'

'In the dark? With no engines? Come on, Davey. It's gone behind a hill. That's all.'

'Then where is it, now, eh? Gone behind another hill? What goes down must come up. If it doesn't come up, it's crashed or it's landed; one or the other.'

Tucky saw the sense in that and they both kept watch, searching the darkness where the lights had vanished. And that's what they were doing when they heard Mr Reynolds' van splashing through the mud by the front gate.

Tucky was downstairs first and threw open the kitchen door. Ann was standing there, taking off her scarf.

'We saw a bomber, Ann. German bomber. We heard it and we saw it. There were lights, Ann, and Davey thinks it's gone down on the moor. There were lights, and they were coming down all the time, then they stopped. We saw it, honest we did, an' the engines were chugging and popping.'

'Tucky, Tucky,' Ann put an arm around him and brought him back into the light of the room. 'Don't be so excited, Tucky. How often do I tell you you must wear shoes on a stone floor? You catch cold that way.'

'What's up, Ann?' Mr Reynolds came in behind her.

'A plane's crashed,' said David simply, getting in before Tucky could start up again. 'It must've been one of the bombers.'

Mr Reynolds smiled. 'I been on searchlight all evening, my dear, and we saw them bombing around Plymouth, but we never saw a plane. No one saw a thing.'

'You missed it,' David said. 'It was out over the

moor and your searchlight was up above the village.'

'Are you certain, Davey?' Mr Reynolds had stopped smiling now. ' 'Tis got to be for certain, y'know.'

'We heard, Mr Reynolds, honest we did,' Tucky said, feeling left out by now. 'It sounded just like the bombers used to sound in London. Just the same.'

Mr Reynolds and Ann looked at each other.

'And the engines were popping, just like Tucky says,' David could see they believed them now.

'Popping?' Ann said. 'What does it mean, this "popping"?'

'Must mean the plane had engine trouble of some sort,' said Mr Reynolds, looking from one boy to the other. 'Could've been hit. Was there any flames? Did you see any flames coming out of her?'

'Just the popping,' Tucky said. 'Then nothing and the lights went out.'

Mr Reynolds bent down and pulled the boys in towards him so that he could look into their faces. 'If there's been a plane down. I'll have to report it. There'll be the army and the police and they'll be wanting to ask you questions, lots of questions. Now think clearly, my dears. It must be for certain. Was there a plane?'

'We saw it, Mr Reynolds,' David said.

'And you're sure it came down over the moor?'

The boys nodded.

'It was there, Mr Reynolds,' said Tucky. 'I promise.'

'They're good boys, Jerry,' Ann said. 'They would not lie.'

'I know that, my dear,' said Mr Reynolds, standing up, 'but the army doesn't know that and neither do the police. They're the ones we'll have to convince. You did well to spot it my dears, and I'll be off back up the village to report it. There won't be much they can do till morning, and they'll be bound to want to see you then. So get off to bed with you both.' Ann went upstairs with them and they watched the glow of the fires on the horizon as Plymouth burned. She made them hot milk and sat on their bed while they drank it.

'It's a terrible thing they do,' she said sadly, gazing out of the window. 'When I was young I watched fires burning in my country, too. It's a terrible thing they do.' She spoke as the boys had never heard her before.

'You're not English, are you, Ann?' David had

wanted to ask her that for a long time, but the moment had never been right.

'I'm French,' Ann said. 'I was French until I married Jerry. Now I am English like you; but I still think of France as my country. Like you, Davey, I know what it is to lose a father in war.' She took their mugs and left the room quickly.

'Now I know why she hates the Germans,' Tucky said quietly, as soon as her footsteps had reached the bottom of the stairs. And later when they were in bed Tucky could not help thinking about it. 'You're lucky.'

'Lucky?'

'If my dad was killed, I'd tell everyone. I'd be proud.'

'I am proud, Tucky. Ann's proud too, but it's better to have a father alive than be proud 'cos he's dead.'

'Depends on your father,' Tucky went on. 'And people like you if your father's dead, like you more anyway.'

'Do you like Ann more 'cos her father's dead?' David said. 'And me? What about me? We were friends years ago.'

'S'pose so,' said Tucky soulfully; and then he thought about the plane again. 'Davey, if that plane crashed like you said, then there'll be men on board.

There'll be Germans. D'you think they'll find them?'

'I hope they're dead,' David said. 'They must've killed hundreds of people in Plymouth tonight. I hope they're dead. They deserve it.'

Neither of them slept much that night, and they heard Mr Reynolds coming back in his van some hours later. David thought of getting out of bed and asking about the plane, about what was being done, but he heard Ann and Mr Reynolds talking together down in the kitchen and somehow he didn't want to see Ann again that night. Tucky got out of bed and tried to listen through the floorboards, but he couldn't make out what they were saying. Then a floorboard creaked and he scrambled back into bed.

It was still dark when Mr Reynolds woke them. He was in his Home Guard uniform. 'The army's downstairs. They want to be out on the moor by daybreak and they want you to come along and show them where it was where you saw the plane. Quick as you can, my dears. We can't go till you're ready.'

The kitchen was full of uniforms, police and soldiers, and they all stood watching them eat down their porridge that Ann insisted they must have before they left. David looked up occasionally from his plate of steaming porridge and recognised some of the faces behind the uniforms. They looked tired and disbelieving. Mr Reynolds was bending over a map with a tall soldier in a peaked cap and a wet macintosh. ' 'Twas out of the bedroom window, sir,' he was saying, 'so it must be in this area here somewhere, almost for certain.'

'But Reynolds,' the officer took off his cap and

shook it, 'there's two observation posts between here and there. Surely if there had been a plane someone else would have spotted it?'

'Not if they were following the searchlight, sir. The boys say the searchlight was sweeping over the village itself at the time.'

The officer turned to face the boys. He had a mean face with a thin moustache that barely covered his top lip. 'You say they're evacuees, Reynolds?'

'That's right, sir. And fine lads they are too, sir. Been with us for three months now. If they say they saw it, then you can be sure they did, sir.'

'Quite so, Reynolds,' said the officer, but he did not sound convinced.

Outside it was a drizzling grey dawn. There was a whole convoy of trucks blocking the lane, and the officer gave the order to get started. Ann wrapped them up in scarves and then they followed Mr Reynolds and clambered into the back of a jeep at the head of the column. The officer with the thin moustache clambered in front and nodded to his driver. 'I hope they're right, Reynolds. There's thirty Home Guard and a whole company from the barracks on this search. I hope you're right.'

David look up nervously at Mr Reynolds who smiled and winked down at him. And Tucky was beginning to wish he'd never told anyone.

Ten times that day the convoy halted and the

soldiers spread out over the moor and disappeared over the hilltops, their rifles hidden under their capes to protect them from the driving rain. The two boys were left behind with the trucks and drivers; and each time the soldiers came back empty-handed they felt worse. The officer kept asking them about the shape of the hills they had seen as the plane came down; he kept pointing up at the hillsides and asking them if they recognised the hilltop. But to the boys all the hills looked alike, and anyway they couldn't remember the hills from the night before, they hadn't even noticed the shape. The officer looked less and less pleased.

The rain cleared a bit after lunch and a spotter plane circled above them all afternoon. The soldiers, some of whom had been quite friendly to start with, now made little attempt to hide their feelings. It was clear what they thought of the 'townies' ' story.

For David and Tucky it was a nightmare. They knew there had been a plane, and they were almost certain it had come down; but each time a search failed and Mr Reynolds clambered wearily back into the deep shaking his head, they began wondering if they had been seeing things that were not there.

By the time the convoy passed the cottage that evening and dropped them off, they knew that everyone thought they had invented the whole story. Even Mr Reynolds seemed dejected.

'Here you are,' said the officer as they jumped out. 'If it was a day off from school they wanted, Reynolds, then they certainly got it.'

'He didn't believe us,' said Tucky rather obviously as the trucks sped off up the lane.

'It's not your fault,' said Mr Reynolds, putting an arm round each of them. 'Maybe the plane wasn't as low as you thought, perhaps it managed to pull up.'

'We could have looked in the wrong places,' David said. 'The moor's a big place.'

'Course we could have, my dear,' said Mr Reynolds, ushering them in the door, 'but I don't think we did.' He didn't sound disbelieving or sarcastic, just weary.

'There was a plane, Mr Reynolds,' Tucky said as they were saying goodnight. 'We saw it, honest we did.'

'Course you did, Tucky. We both know you did,

don't we Ann? Off you go now; it's been a long day, you're tired, I'm tired and Ann is certainly tired. She's done the farm all by herself today. Let's think no more about it.'

But they did think about it; they thought about little else all week. Everyone in the village had heard about the search and at school the 'townies' were not allowed to forget about it. Everyone had made up his mind: the 'townies' had got themselves off school for a day by calling out the Home Guard, the army and a spotter plane on some cock-and-bull story about a bomber coming down on the moor. Tucky was not the warlike type, but he very nearly got himself in a fight when someone suggested it might have been a flying saucer they'd seen and that they'd all better keep their eyes open for little men from Mars. Mr Cooper stopped it just in time, but none the less people laughed about it openly, and for the first time since they came to the village David and Tucky felt alone again and separate from the other children.

Time and time again they went over what they had seen that night, and time and time again they convinced themselves it had been a plane, that the engines had been spluttering and that it had been going down when the lights vanished. But every time they had to reconcile all that with the fact that no plane had been found, and all the reasoning in the world could not change that.

Ann tried hard to console them at home, explaining how easy it was to make mistakes, how often eyes could deceive.

'But we heard it as well, Ann. Both of us did,' said David.

Mr Reynolds stood up from the tea table and put on his hat. 'You still think there's a plane up there, don't you?'

'I know there is,' David replied.

'But we searched all day, Davey. There was nothing there.'

'Can't we try? Tucky stood up. 'Can't we go and look for ourselves? I think we went too far away with the soldiers. It wasn't that far away. We heard those engines as if they were just over the cottage. I remember the windows shook.'

'Please, Mr Reynolds,' David added his support. 'Just one last chance, please.'

'All right, my dears, but I'll not be able to come with you. I've left the farm for one day this week, and there's still a mass of work to catch up on. Farm doesn't work itself y'know and I can't leave it all to Ann now, can I?'

'It's Saturday tomorrow,' said Ann. 'It is lovely on the moor when it's fine, like it was today, and even if you don't find your plane, it would be a good walk anyway, no?'

'Only if it's fine, mind,' Mr Reynolds added, 'and you're not to go anywhere we haven't been together already. You'll have to turn around by midday. I don't want to call the army out again to come looking for you two on the moor. They may not be very keen to find you anyway.'

'Will they be safe, Jerry?' Ann looked worried.

'We've been up there often enough, I think. If the weather's right, they'll manage. I've told them and warned them often enough. 'Tis summer now, there's not much can go wrong if they stick to the tracks.'

It was fine again the next day, and the final search was on. It was still wet under foot as they tramped across the fields, but as soon as they reached the lower slopes of the moor, they felt the spring of the turf under their boots, and the higher they climbed the drier it became.

They navigated by following the line of the highest tor they could see from the bedroom window. The plane had vanished somewhere in line with that. 'Yes Tor' Mr Reynolds had called it.

Tucky was stronger and went on ahead, setting a fast pace, while David kept him going in the right direction from behind. They climbed rocky river valleys following the streams, but always when they had struggled up one valley there was another beyond, and Yes Tor seemed to have come no closer. At every hilltop they paused to catch their breath and search the vast emptiness of the moor. There were sheep enough, and they recognised the red mark of Hamleigh Farm they had marked Mr Reynolds' sheep with. Occasionally a group of sturdy brown ponies came in close to them but moved away as they approached them. But there was no aeroplane and no German pilots.

Sweaty and tired, they sat on top of a cairn eating the sandwiches Ann had made for them. The early optimism of the morning had gone, and the flies would not leave them alone. David looked at the watch Ann had lent him.

'After eleven already. An hour more and we'll have to give up and turn round.'

'Not worth going on,' said Tucky. 'We'll never find it, because it's not here. It never did crash. They're right, there's nothing here. Let's go back and forget about it.'

'One more hour, Tucky, that's all. Then we'll turn back, all right? We've come this far, we might as well finish it. There's a chance.' David was just as dejected as Tucky, but the thought of those children at school laughing at them next week, the thought of the look on their faces if they did find something – that was enough to drive him on.

At mid-day, under a blazing sun, having nothing but a few lizards in sight, they finally turned round and headed back towards the farm. Both of them had given up now, but David was still not going to admit it. As a matter of course they still searched the valleys and hills around them, but they were just retracing their steps and all hope had gone. They wanted only to get off the moor and forget the whole business.

As far as possible they followed the same tracks, but they took some short cuts as they trudged back down the hills, recognising landmarks ahead and making straight for them across country. On the way out they had kept close to the paths Mr

Reynolds had shown them, but on the way back nothing seemed to matter any more and they just wanted the quickest route home.

David was leading by now, and Tucky trailed behind him, dispirited and silent. But it was Tucky who suggested that instead of following the river to the stepping stones at the foot of the valley, they might as well cross higher up and cut off over the moor.

Tucky was first in the water, holding his boots and socks up above his head. 'S'easy,' he said. 'Come on, you can do it.'

'Too fast for me,' said David, watching the water foaming furiously round Tucky's legs. 'I'll go on down to the stepping stones and cross there, like before.' David wasn't scared, it was just a feeling that the water looked too fast as it whipped round the rocks. Tucky was jumping from stone to stone, and when he got to the middle he turned round and waited for David to join him. David managed it to the middle and they stood on the rock and looked at the gap they had to jump.

'I'll go first,' Tucky shouted over the roar of the water. The gap yawned wide, frothing and swirling, but Tucky leapt and landed easily enough on the plateau of rock on the other side. He turned, balancing precariously, and beckoned David. David screwed himself up for the jump, trying not to look down into the water.

'Jump upwards,' he said to himself. Once he nearly went but he held back at the last moment.

'Come on, Davey. You can do it. Just jump.'

David took a deep breath and jumped, but his foot slipped behind him on the rock and he fell forward into the water. He heard Tucky shouting, and looked up to see his out-stretched hand. His feet struck out in panic and the water pulled him away. His fingers reached out for the rock above him, but then the water closed in over him and he was dragged irresistibly downwards. He tried to cough the water out of his lungs, but more was coming in all the time and he couldn't seem to do it. He came up once into the brightness of the sun and Tucky was running along the bank screaming something at him. Then the water whisked him round, his back thudded into a rock and he was underwater again, and his boots seemed heavy.

Then he remembered he could not swim, and it came to him coldly that if he could not swim, then he would drown. He screamed in his terror and the water poured into his mouth cutting him short. The more he kicked the deeper down he went. He came up again, arms flailing. Tucky was standing there watching, his mouth wide open.

An arm was around his neck and another under

his shoulders, and he was being dragged back against the force of the water. He struggled, but the grip tightened fiercely and he was pushed under the water. I'm drowning, he thought, and Tucky's just standing there. He can swim, I've seen him at Birchington. Why doesn't he help me? Why doesn't Tucky help?

CHAPTER 5

THE SUN WAS DAZZLING HIS EYES AND TUCKY was leaning over him. From somewhere there was the smell of wood smoke.

'Davey! Davey! Can you hear me? You all right?' Tucky seemed to be shouting, but David heard him only faintly at first. 'We were right, Davey. It *was* a bomber, a German bomber, and there's two of them here.'

'Two?'

'Two German pilots. One's hurt but the other one pulled you out of the river.'

David pushed himself up slowly and propped himself on his elbows. The smoke came from a fire a few feet away, and beyond that up against a low dry stone wall there were two men in blue

uniforms. One of them stood up now and came towards them. There was the black but of a revolver sticking out of his belt, and David saw that he was unshaven. He was wearing only a shirt and trousers and they were clinging wet. He crouched down a few paces away.

'Your friend is well now?' He spoke haltingly, with a heavy accent. 'He is better?'

'You tell him, mister,' Tucky said excitedly. 'You tell him. You're a German, aren't you?'

The man nodded. 'We are German, yes.'

'See, Davey. There was a plane and it did crash.'

'You were in that plane?' David was trying to take it all in.

'It was my plane, yes. We were hit and then we lost power. We had to crash-land.' His eyes were sunk deep in his head, and his hair was still wet.

'You were bombing Plymouth?' David asked. He could feel a knot of anger building up inside him. The man nodded slowly.

'Their plane sank,' Tucky went on. 'That's what he told me. Landed in a bog. Remember Mr Reynolds telling us that story of a horse and rider that were sucked down – that's what happened to their plane. That's what he said.'

'And they've been out here all week?' David said, looking past the fire to the man by the wall.

'S'pose so,' said Tucky. 'That's one's hurt his leg or something, doesn't speak any English.'

David looked at them both. There was nothing threatening or frightening about them, they were just two exhausted, pale-looking men with sad eyes and kind faces. They were faces he should hate. Perhaps these were the men who had shot down his father over the French coast and cheered as they watched him crashing into the beaches. These were the men who had bombed London and Plymouth and killed thousands. Yet one of them had saved his life.

'He took your clothes off, Davey, after he dragged you out. They've over there by the fire. Should be dry soon, you were unconscious long enough.' David had been aware of a roughness against his skin, but it was only now that he realised he was covered in a dark blue overcoat. His clothes were hanging over a frame of sticks by the fire.

'My friend is not well,' the German said. 'He cannot move much and he is cold. I need food – food and blankets. The nights are cold here and he coughs. Will you help us, please?'

'Help you!' David was almost shouting. He pulled himself to his feet, gathering the greatcoat around him. 'Help you? After what you've done? You come here bombing and killing and you want us to help!'

'It is a war,' he replied sadly. 'In war people die – on both sides.'

'Why don't you give yourself up?' Tucky said. 'You can't escape, not if your friend can't move. And there are soldiers out looking for you, you know. We told them about your plane.'

The German threw more wood on the fire. 'Perhaps you are right,' he said, 'but we must try. We need time to recover. Two days ago we have finished the emergency food. We have nothing left – just water from the river. This is the first fire I have dared to light. We must keep warm, and we must have food. Then we will escape over the moor to the sea and find a boat.'

'What about the soldiers?' said Tucky.

'They did not find us last time. It is a big place to search, this moor.'

'And what if we tell them where you are?' David said, as defiantly as he could.

'Then we shall be caught, my young friend. I cannot move my friend any more now, and I cannot leave him. We are in your hands,' and he turned away and walked back to his friend on the other side of the fire.

'What do we do?' Tucky whispered. 'We got to help him, haven't we? He saved your life, Davey, pushed all the water out of you and he was risking a lot to light that fire for you. You owe him, Davey. We both do.'

'He's a German, isn't he? He's probably bombed over London. What if it was his bombs that hit the Perkins' house back in Islington, eh? How many d'you think he's killed?'

'But he saved your life, Davey. He needn't have done it. He could have let you drown.'

As soon as his clothes were dry enough to put on, David got dressed. The two Germans watched from their wall. David walked over and handed back the greatcoat. 'Thank you,' he said. The taller airman, the one who had saved him, took it and laid it over his friend.

'If you come back,' he said, 'please bring us food. If you send the soldiers, then goodbye.'

David turned away and the two boys left them

sitting there, and when they turned round farther down the valley, they saw a great puff of white smoke going up. The fire was being put out. It was still a long walk back to the farm, an hour at least, and all that time they talked about what they should do. Every instinct except one told them to give the Germans up, to call in the soldiers, to tell Mr Reynolds. After all, wouldn't Ann and Mr Reynolds be pleased? Wouldn't the laughing faces in the village be silenced? Wouldn't their stock be high at school? And wouldn't everyone have to eat their words about the 'townies'? And apart from that, they were Germans, enemies; it was a duty to make sure they were captured.

It was Tucky who did most of the talking. He kept on reminding David that the German had saved his life, that you couldn't turn on someone who had saved your life, no matter who he was, but David was determined. He would tell Mr Reynolds as soon as they got back, and leave it to him. By the time they reached the cottage, he was longing to break the news.

Ann met them at the door. 'Where have you been, you two? I was worried?' Then she caught sight of David's clothes. 'Davey, what has

happened?' She reached out and felt his shirt. 'It is damp. What has happened?'

'I fell in the river,' David started to explain. 'We'd almost given up, Ann. We were crossing the river and I fell in, slipped on the rocks, and then . . .'

'Lucky I was with him, Ann, I can tell you. The river wasn't that fast, and it's not too deep there either. Still, s'lucky I was with him.' Tucky smiled up at Ann. David was about to interrupt, but Tucky went on before he had the chance. 'And he can't swim. He slipped on the rocks and I leapt in after him and fished him out. Wet as a kipper, he was. No doubt about it, lucky I was there,' and he preened himself, flashed a grin at David and went into the cottage. It was a brilliant performance.

David just stood there, gaping after him. He had known Tucky a very long time, and Tucky had never surprised him before; that was what he liked about Tucky, he could always tell what Tucky was thinking, what he was going to do. Until now, that is.

Ann put an arm round his shoulder. 'Are you all right, Davey? You look as if you have seen a ghost. Are you cold still?'

'Yes, I'm cold,' was all he could say.

There was a steaming hot bath and tea in the kitchen, and then Ann went off to help Mr Reynolds with the milking. It was the first time the boys had been left alone, the first chance they had had to talk. David didn't waste any time. 'We agreed. We said we'd tell them. We must tell them.'

'I never agreed anything,' said Tucky, ready for him. 'You tell them if you like, but I can tell you, if someone had just risked his own life to save mine, I wouldn't kick him in the teeth – German or not, it doesn't matter.'

'But we can't, Tucky. We can't help Germans to escape, it's not right. We're supposed to be fighting them. We can't.'

'Like I say,' Tucky said firmly. 'You owe them, and what's more you know you do. All he's asking for is some food and blankets – if you don't think that's a fair exchange for saving your life, then I think it's a pity he went in after you.'

David had never heard Tucky like this. He was excitable, yes; impetuous, yes; but he'd never found him determined or single-minded.

Tucky leaned towards him over the kitchen table. 'I like you, Davey. We've been best friends ever since I can remember. You always seemed to do right by people. You've done right by me, been a real friend since we left home, but if you turn those Germans in just because your father ...'

'My father?'

'That's what it is, Davey, isn't it? And maybe Ann's father as well. They're Germans and the Germans killed your dad, so you hate them all, don't you, every one of them?'

There was not a single word Tucky had spoken that David could argue with. Tucky was right. He did owe the Germans out on the moor.

'All right,' he conceded. 'We'll do it, but not for long.'

Tucky smiled like his old self for the first time since they had got back. They didn't see Mr Reynolds again that evening; he was busy fencing at the bottom of Front Meadow. But next morning over breakfast, before David and Tucky left for school, he heard all about their search on the moor. 'So, you found nothing,' he smiled wryly, 'and Davey here fell in the river.'

'I slipped, Mr Reynolds. Those stones were all slimy.'

'You crossed at the stepping stones, like I said?'

'Yes, Mr Reynolds.'

'And no sign of that plane?'

'Nothing,' said Tucky. 'We must have made a mistake. P'raps it went up again, behind a hill or something, and we just didn't see it. Sorry, Mr Reynolds.'

'Never you mind, my dear. You were right to tell us if you thought you saw it. Everyone makes mistakes, and anyway 'twas good practice for the army and for us – even if no one enjoyed it much. We won't mention it again. Off you go now, you'll be late for school.'

School was still buzzing with the 'townies" shot-down German bomber, and David and Tucky longed to blurt out their secret. 'Haven't you found it yet, Davey boy?' and 'Look out, the Luftwaffe's about!' And whenever Mr Cooper wanted someone with a good imagination, he turned to the 'townies' with a knowing smile, and everyone laughed.

It was a wretched day, only made bearable by the knowledge that they knew they were right. On the way back home that afternoon, they worked out their plan.

'Whatever happens, Mr Reynolds and Ann must never find out. Never,' said David. 'Nothing must be missed.'

'What about the blankets? They'll miss those, won't they? They're bound to.'

'Not if we take two off our bed,' said David. 'We make our own beds, don't we? No one'll miss them, 'cept us. We can bring them back after they've gone. No one need notice.'

'What about the food then?'

'There's eggs,' David had thought it all out. 'We can get them from the chicken hut soon as we get back. Then there's carrots and radishes in the vegetable patch – I've seen Ann pulling them up often enough. I know where they are.'

'That won't be enough.'

'Then there's that bowl of bread and leftovers that Ann keeps on the window ledge above the sink. We could take that, some of it anyway. No one would miss that – 'cept the pigs, of course.'

David had been planning it all day, and once they got home, he knew exactly what had to be done. He sent Tucky upstairs for the blankets while he went for the food. As he expected, Ann was out with Mr Reynolds haymaking across the stream by Long Close; it was far enough away from the house for it to be safe. They wrapped the food in one of the blankets and made off out of the back door, and across the fields towards the moors.

Once off the farm they kept to the cover of the hedgerows until they reached the open moor and were out of sight of the cottage. Tucky flopped down behind a stone wall and waited for David to join him. He fought to catch his breath, hanging his head back and taking in great gulps of air. David slumped down next to him and checked that the food was still inside the blankets. One egg had broken, but everything was there. It was then they heard someone coming up the track behind them. They looked at each other in alarm. The panting was close now, just the other side of the stone wall. The froze against it, rigid and frightened. And then Jip came lolloping into sight, saw them cowering there and trotted over, tail wagging, tongue hanging down from his pink and grinning mouth. They laughed themselves silly with relief.

'Dogs can't tell tales,' David said, and Jip followed them along over the hills to where the river tumbled over the rocks. They crossed over the stepping stones and clambered on up, always looking ahead of them to see if the Germans were still there. They approached the place slowly, but Jip ran on ahead sniffing the ground busily, alternately growling and yapping in excitement. He disappeared behind the stone wall, and then there was silence.

The German airmen were where they had left them, only closer in among the rocks. One of them held Jip under his arm, his hand clamped over his muzzle. Both wore their blue greatcoats and were crouching down low. Their faces relaxed and the black revolver that was pointing at the boys was lowered.

'Is it your dog?' he asked. David nodded, and the Germans released Jip and patted his neck gently. Jip sprang away and cowered behind the boys. 'Food? Have you brought food?' David handed over the blanket, and the two Germans spread it out carefully in front of them. They divided it equally and then devoured it like starved dogs, looking up from time to time as if someone might take it away from them.

The boys looked on in silence, wondering how anyone could be that hungry. They ate anything and everything – meat fat, cold porridge, stale bread, peelings, carrots, raw eggs. When they had finished not a crumb was left on the blanket – except the eggshells. They sat back against the wall, breathing deeply.

'That was good, very good,' the airman was panting. 'Gurt here, he slept hardly at all, it will be good for him. You are kind, very kind. Thank you, it was a feast, a real feast.'

The boys saw that the men had built themselves a rough shelter up against the wall since the day before. It was made of wooden supports, and covered in bracken, dried grass and freshly cut turf. There was more bracken on the floor inside and enough room for both men to squeeze in together. 'It's not a palace, my young friend,' he said, 'but it is better than nothing.' The German smiled quietly as he spoke, but then his face altered suddenly.

They all heard it together, the drone of an aeroplane, and it was coming closer all the time. The two Germans crawled in under their shelter and pulled the blankets in after them. Tucky spotted it first as it came over the hill, a single-engined spotter plane, a biplane, and it flew down towards them over the moor, its RAF markings plainly visible. It was the same spotter plane that had been used in the search the week before.

CHAPTER 6

'WAVE,' DAVID SHOUTED. 'WAVE AT HIM.' AND
Tucky obeyed instinctively, waving after the plane as
it banked and came in for a second run. David gave
the thumbs-up sign and the 'V' for victory. 'Look
happy, Tucky, smile at him.'

The spotter plane swept down even lower this
time, and they could see the pilot waving back at
them, and the two boys waved after it as it waggled
its wings in salute. Tucky glanced down at the
Germans' shelter, but there was no sign of them, and
by the time he looked up again, the plane was
climbing fast over the moor and turnings towards the
south.

'What if they saw?' Tucky tugged at David's elbow.

'What if they saw the Germans?'

'They didn't, they couldn't have.' David was almost sure. 'We're two boys out with our dog on the moor, nothing wrong in that, is there?'

'And that shelter, what about the shelter?'

David didn't have the time to answer. 'So, you told them about us.' The boys swung round at the sound of the German's voice. He was standing up by the shelter, his greatcoat pulled up under his chin.

'No, mister, we didn't tell no one. Honest.' Tucky sounded frightened.

'Honest?' He came towards them. 'And the plane? The plane was not sent? You told no one?'

'No one,' said David firmly, moving closer to Tucky. 'We kept it a secret. I didn't want to, but he did, and we told no one.'

'But you were waving,' the airman went on. 'You wanted them to see you, to see us.'

David shook his head. 'Do you think we'd want to be caught giving food and blankets to Germans? Do you? We were waving to show them we weren't in any trouble. That's all.'

He looked hard at both of them, and then went back to the shelter to talk with his friend who had crawled out by now. For some minutes they talked agitatedly in German, and the boys stood and waited. Finally he came back towards them.

'You are right,' he said. 'I am sorry it is like this for you. My friend, Gurt, he says we should trust you. He says you have already done enough to pay me for yesterday. He says we should not ask you to help your country's enemies. You would have trouble if you were caught, no?' David nodded. 'We just ask you one more thing. Then no more. Tomorrow we will try to cross the moor to the sea. My friend is no better. His cough is worse, and his leg is not good, but we must try. We need one more day to gain our strength. We need one more good meal, and some drink – brandy perhaps, to keep us warm inside. Can you do this for us?'

David and Tucky looked at each other. 'This'll be the last?' said David. 'There'll be no more?'

'You have my word. It is the last.'

'All right, mister. We got to go now. We'll be back this time tomorrow,' and David whistled for Jip who was sniffing the blankets. 'Come on, Jip.'

'Thank you again, my friends,' the German said, and his friend by the shelter smiled weakly and waved his thanks.

The boys were at the bottom of the valley before either of them spoke, and Jip was running on ahead chasing every scent he found. 'Not so bad, are they Davey? For Germans, I mean?'

'Brandy,' David muttered. 'And where do they think we're going to get brandy from?'

'There's some bottles under the stairs,' said Tucky. 'Where Mr Reynolds gets his cider from.'

'Steal them, you mean. We've got to steal from Ann and Mr Reynolds?'

'We stole the eggs, didn't we?' said Tucky.

'That's different,' said David, and he felt uncomfortable as he said it.

Mr Reynolds was out on Home Guard duty again by the time they got back, and they helped Ann feed the stock and shut them up for the night. 'Not many eggs,' Ann said as they were crossing the yard. David and Tucky said nothing. 'Twice as many yesterday, something must have frightened them. Jerry said there might be a fox about. And I left the bowl of slops for the pigs on the ledge above the sink – just like always. You did not move it, did you boys?'

'Probably Jip,' David said quickly. 'He's always at the dustbins and things. He's taken them before, hasn't he?'

'Strange, though,' Ann went on.

'What is?' Tucky was nervous, and he showed it.

'You could be right, Jip does take the slops sometimes, but he doesn't put the bowl back on the kitchen table when he has finished.'

'That yellow bowl?' David asked. 'I found it outside in the yard, Ann. It was upside down by the trough, so I put it back in the kitchen.' David hadn't the courage to look at Ann as he spoke. She seemed happy with his explanation, and forgot all about it. But at supper she reminded Jerry about the fox. 'I think it must be that, Jerry. They are not laying away, and they're eating as good as ever. Must be the fox.'

Mr Reynolds was still in his uniform, and unbuttoned his tunic. 'Course it could be, but 'tis the early spring they come after the fowls, when there's cubs to feed. 'Tis a bit late now, and I haven't seen him about for weeks the old fox, he's a cunning old devil. He doesn't come after the fowls on a bright summer's day; he waits till the wind's up high, and comes around dusk. That's when you want to watch out for the fox. Old devil, he is. No, they've gone off the lay – they do it from time to time. Get a bit lazy,

just the same as we do.' He sniffed the air greedily and rubbed his hands. 'That's smells good enough, Ann my dear.'

'I made that potato pie with eggs, but there will not be enough egg, not as much as there should be.'

Mr Reynolds leaned up against the cooking stove and warmed his hands on the pipes. ' 'Tis the coldest place on God's earth, that moor. Even in high summer, the evenings are like winter. 'Tis terrible. Still 'twas a good exercise, very good.'

'Up on the moor?' David's heart seemed to come up to his mouth.

' 'Twas after our little caper last week, my dear, the

good Captain thought we should have more practice at searching up there. So up we went – and 'twas a good thing we did, too.'

'What d'you mean?' David thought he would choke on his mouthful.

'Did you find anything?' Tucky asked, all the colour drained from his face.

'Course we did. If the Home Guard goes out on a search, you can be sure they find something.'

'What did you find, Jerry? Don't keep on. You're teasing,' said Ann, laughing.

'No planes, my dears, no Germans, I'm afraid, just two of my sheep stuck fast in a bog.' Mr Reynolds' face wrinkled into a smile. 'Poor little devils, been like that all day by the state of them; right up over their backs it was. You'd think the sheep would know where to go and where not to go, wouldn't you?' The boys laughed with Ann, in a desperate attempt to hide their relief.

Once in bed that night, the boys lay still, listening to the talk downstairs, listening for any sign that Ann or Mr Reynolds was suspicious.

'Do you think they know?' Tucky whispered.

'Not yet. Don't think so.'

'I saw those bottles under the stairs like I said.

There's loads of them, Davey. They won't notice if one's missing.'

'Won't they?' David was sullen.

'When shall we take one?' Tucky shifted up on his elbow.

'Why don't you go and ask them if you're in such a hurry?' David snapped angrily. 'Why don't you go down and tell them we're looking after two Germans on the moor, and would they mind if we took a bottle of brandy to keep them warm and help them to escape.'

Tucky was silent for a moment. 'No need to have a go at me, Davey.'

'Well, it was your idea, wasn't it?' David hissed.

'S'pose so.' Tucky lay down again. 'But we had to do it, Davey. We got to do it.'

'Why?'

' 'Cos we said we would, that's why.'

'And Ann and Mr Reynolds. Have you thought what we're going to say if they find out what we've done? What are we going to tell them, Tucky?'

'I dunno,' said Tucky. 'I hope they never find out, 'cos I dunno.'

School was slow the next day. Every lesson

dragged on, and it seemed as if the last bell would never ring. For Tucky it was spent wondering about the two airmen up on the moor, hoping no one else would discover them, and speculating whether or not they'd make it to the sea. David could think of nothing but the brandy, about how he was going to steal from two of the best people in the world to help the same people who had killed his father. He hated what he was doing, and dreaded having to do it.

Ann and Mr Reynolds were out turning the hay as they came back up the lane. Mr Reynolds was waving his rake, calling to them to come over. He was leaning up against the cart wiping the sweat away from his eyes. 'Got a job for you two,' he said. 'Jip's gone off, my dears. I was up on the moor this morning turning out the late lambs and Jip took it in his head to run off. I nearly went after him, but while the weather's right I thought I'd best get on with this. Course he'll find his way back himself like as not, but I'd be happier if you'd go out and find him. He made off in the direction of the river I think.' He stopped and looked closely at David. 'What's the matter, Davey? You don't look too good.'

'Nothing,' said David hurriedly.

'We'll find him, Mr Reynolds,' said Tucky. 'We were going up on the moor anyway, weren't we, Davey?'

'Don't be late for supper,' Ann called after them.

They ran back to the cottage first and dropped their school things in the bedroom. Tucky pulled off his pillowcase. 'We can use this to carry the food,' he said.

'You know where Jip went, don't you, Tucky? He went off to see them. What if Mr Reynolds had followed him? They've got a gun, haven't they?'

'They'd never use it, would they?' Tucky said. 'They never used it on us. They're not like that. They wouldn't have hurt him, and anyway, it never happened. Stop worrying about it. Come on.'

Tucky was impatient to get out there and he went off in search of food with strict instructions from David to take nothing that would be missed. David made sure Ann and Mr Reynolds were still out in the field and then went downstairs to find the brandy. He sorted through the bottles under the stairs, looking over his shoulders every few seconds to make sure no one was coming. He felt like a thief in the night. There was no brandy, only a bottle of whisky, hall full, and crates and crates of empties. He took the whisky and tucked it under his shirt.

They met at the door and ran, Tucky holding the pillowcase in front of him and David clutching the whisky in both hands as he tried to keep up with Tucky. They reached the stone wall again, and flopped down behind it.

'Look,' Tucky panted, opening up the pillowcase. 'Look what I got.' There were eggs again, two tins of corned beef and the remains of the pie from the evening before.

'You're mad, Tucky, why d'you take that?'

'That's all there was, honest. There were masses of tins like this and I left some of the pie in the bowl. There was nothing in the slops bowl. S'all I could find, Davey.'

It was clouding over now, and the hills on the moor were changing colour. The stones took on a deeper granite grey, and the grass turned almost purple on the hillsides. As they clambered up the hill towards the Germans' hide they felt the first drop of rain. But this time they felt something was wrong. It was all too quiet. They called out for Jip, but there was no answering bark.

The hide was deserted, the shelter had disappeared

as if it had never been there. Only the damp grey ashes by the stone wall were left to show that anyone had been there at all.

CHAPTER 7

THE BOYS STOOD IN THE DRIZZLE CALLING
and whistling for Jip, and then from high up on the
hills came a familiar barking. It seemed to be coming
from the cairn, a massive pile of granite rocks that
dominated the valley like some prehistoric fortress.
Tucky whistled again, and back came Jip's reassuring
bark; and then they saw him standing up on the cairn
against the sky, his body shaking as he barked. Tucky
set off up the hill with David in close pursuit; and Jip
jumped down from the rocks and bounced down
towards them, tail bobbing, tongue hanging out.

It was a long climb up. They had to make
frequent detours to find the safest way to the top,
zigzagging up the hill towards the cairn. Jip could

climb where they could not and ran on ahead, turning every so often to make sure they were following.

Tucky stopped to catch his breath and shouted up, 'You up there? We got your food.' For some moments there was no response.

'Come up.' It was the German's voice from behind the rocks. There was no doubt about that. Tucky waited for David and they went on up together.

It was a small grassy clearing encircled by great boulders, and in one corner a great granite slab had fallen across the walls to form a roof. It reminded David of pictures he'd seen of Stonehenge, only smaller. One German was lying down under the roof, covered in blankets, and the other stood beside him stroking Jip.

'We thought you'd gone,' Tucky said. 'You didn't tell us you were moving.'

'The plane that came over yesterday,' he said. 'I thought it could have seen us. It was a good thing. There were soldiers out yesterday, just the other side of the river. We are safe here now.'

David was looking at the other airman, who was struggling to sit up. 'Your friend? Is he worse?'

'Not good, not good. He is very ill. You have brought the brandy?'

'Whisky,' said David. 'There was no brandy.' He handed him the bottle.

'Thank you, my friend,' the German's face broke into a half smile. 'It will be a help.' He was even paler than the day before, and his beard had grown darker. He knelt down beside his friend and helped him to sit up. He tilted the bottle and the boys watched the injured German drink it as if it was water. Twice his whole body was shaken by violent coughing fits, but still he came back for more until finally he pushed it away. He leant back against the rocks, nodded at the two boys and smiled his thanks. Tucky put the pillowcase down inside the shelter and stood back.

'We won't bring any more,' David said suddenly when they had finished emptying the pillowcase. They ate on as if he had said nothing, ripping open the tins of corned beef and shovelling the meat directly from the tins into their mouths. David said it louder. 'We have done enough. There won't be any more. You understand?'

The German nodded as he finished his mouthful and wiped his mouth with the back of his sleeve.

'You have done more than enough. It is good that we can help each other in these sad times. It is good.'

'We only did it 'cos you helped us,' David said. 'That's all. We're still enemies.'

'No, I don't think so,' he looked up at them and smiled. 'I am wearing the uniform of your enemy, but we are not enemies, not any more.'

'We must take Jip now,' David said, wanting it to be over. 'We were sent out to find Jip. We've got to get back.'

The airman got to his feet slowly, holding out his hand to stop them. 'Please,' he said, 'there is one last thing.'

'No,' David was almost shouting. 'It's finished. I've paid you back, haven't I? We won't do any more, do you understand? No more.'

'Please.' The German took a step closer, and the boys backed away. 'We want no more food, no more anything.'

'Come on, Tucky.' David turned to go. 'I'm going.'

'I want you to take my friend back with you,' said the German quietly. 'As your prisoner. He has agreed. He is not well enough to go with me over the moor. I hoped food and warmth would help, but it hasn't. He wishes to go with you as your prisoner.'

'You want us to take him? Hand him over to the army?' Tucky said. Pictures of him leading a captured German pilot through the village, with crowds cheering and church bells pealing, came swarming into his mind. Their faces! The look on their faces!

'How far it is?' the German asked.

'How far?' David was still trying to take it in.

'To your home, your village?'

'It's not our home exactly,' he said. 'We're evacuees.'

'From London, mister, to get away from the bombs,' Tucky answered for him.

The man nodded knowingly, and looked hard at David. 'From London. I am sorry, my friends. Perhaps when you are older you will understand that we all do things we know we should not do. But perhaps you have learnt that already.'

David looked away. 'It takes over an hour,' he said. 'But it's downhill most of the way.'

'To begin with I will go with you – Gurt, my friend, he cannot walk too far – I will come to help carry him. He is a big man, too heavy for you, I think. You will take him?'

'We will, won't we Davey?' Tucky was eager.

'All right,' David said. 'But no one must see you. You won't make it, you know.'

'Make it?'

'Over the moor. It's thirty miles of hills, bogs and rivers, and the army trains all over it. They'll catch you, and if they don't, the moor will kill you.'

'Will you tell them about me?'

David shook his head. 'There's no need. Mr Reynolds says no one can cross the moor from north to south without a map or a compass, and without knowing the moor. You'll never do it.'

'In planes we navigate by the stars,' he said. 'The moor may be big, but it is not as big as the sky. I will try anyway. I have to try. If you were away from home, and you wanted to get back, you would try, wouldn't you?'

They started off down the hill, Jip prancing on ahead sniffing at every rabbit hole. Tucky carried both the blankets over his shoulder, and kept looking round every few yards to make sure the two Germans were still behind them. David stuffed the pillowcase inside his jumper and wondered how they were going to explain away the blankets to Mr Reynolds. The deception was getting too complicated; something must go wrong, he was sure of it.

The boys found themselves walking too fast for the airmen, who needed to stop to rest from time to time. The injured one was being carried, slung over his friend's shoulder in a fireman's lift. David and Tucky sat down on a rock to wait for them to catch up. It was still drizzling and the German found it difficult to keep his feet as he came down towards them. He plodded on past them, and David saw the effort on his face and a look of grim determination.

'What're we going to say?'

David had made up his mind. 'We bumped into them by accident. No need to lie any more, Tucky.'

'That's just it,' Tucky went on. 'There's two of them, and we're only bringing one of them in. What're you going to do about the other one? Are we going to tell them or what?'

'I don't know.' David got up and followed the Germans.

David stopped them when they reached the low stone wall that separated the moor from the farm, and here the airman lowered his friend gently on to his feet. They talked to each other briefly in German, and then shook hands solemnly.

'You will look after him, please?' he said. 'He needs a doctor. You will make sure he has a doctor?'

'Course we will,' Tucky said excitedly. 'Course we will, won't we, Davey?' And David nodded his agreement.

'So, he is your prisoner now,' and he felt deep into the inside of his coat and pulled out the black revolver. 'You will need this,' he said, handing it to David. It was cold and heavy, heavier than David had imagined. 'It is loaded, but the safety catch is on. Be careful with it, please.' David balanced it in his hand and gripped the butt, his finger curling round the trigger.

'I could make you come too,' he said.

'Of course, Davey.' The man nodded. 'But friends do not use guns on each other.' He held out his hand to David. David looked down at the outstretched hand and took it. 'Goodbye, Davey, and you too, Tucky. Auf Wiedersehen.'

'Bye,' said David.

'And good luck,' Tucky shouted after him. But the

German was striding away into the rain, head bent forward, the collar of his coat turned up to cover his neck.

Mr Reynolds was in the yard, bringing in the sows. He heard footsteps behind him, and then Jip was nuzzling his leg. 'So you little devil, you. You found him then, my dears.' He still had not turned round. 'Dogs are like horses, got minds of their own.'

'We found him, Mr Reynolds,' said Tucky. 'And someone else. Look.'

Mr Reynolds turned and stared. 'Your plane? From your plane, is he?' he could hardly believe what he was looking at.

'Jip found him, Mr Reynolds,' said David. 'He's a German bomber pilot – Luftwaffe.'

'I can see that, my dear, I can see that.' He looked the German up and down, and then he noticed the revolver David was holding in his hand. 'Now, you give that thing to me, my dear,' he said, and he walked round the German, keeping his distance, and took the revolver from David. 'Ann,' he called out, not taking his eyes off the German. 'Ann, come here. Come out here.' He was pointing the revolver at the German now and waving him towards the cottage.

'Your plane, must've been your plane, 'most for certain. You were right, my dears, right after all. Does he speak English?'

'No,' Tucky said. He was longing to see Ann's face when she saw.

'He's limping, isn't he? Course he's been out on the moor for the best part of a week; no, 'twould be more now, wouldn't it? Looks half starved, doesn't he? Ann!'

Ann threw open the door and came running out, her hands white with flour. She stopped dead and her hand shot to her mouth.

'German pilot,' Tucky said. 'From our plane. We found him out on the moor.'

'Jip found him,' David said quickly.

'Did he hurt you?' Ann had gone white.

'Gentle as a lamb, by the look of him,' said Mr Reynolds.

'But the gun,' said Ann. 'The gun. How did you get the gun?'

'Just gave himself up,' David said. 'He can hardly walk, Ann; he's tired out and coughing; he should see a doctor.'

'The van, my dear, get the van out,' said Mr

Reynolds. 'Take it up to the village and get Captain Starey, and if he's not there, then ring up the army at Okehampton. They'll send someone out, but quick as you can now. We'll look after him here, won't we, my dears?'

Ann came closer to the German and looked up into his face. 'Just people, just ordinary people, like you and me,' she said.

In the warmth of the kitchen, the German sat in Ann's chair by the stove, holding a mug of tea in his hands, and shivering. Mr Reynolds nursed the revolver, shaking his head.

'And the blankets, I don't understand about the blankets,' he said slowly. 'They're ours, no doubt about that. That green one, I've seen that one on my bed before now, most for certain. 'Twas on my bed for years.'

'We found all sorts up there,' David spoke up confidently. 'We brought them all back, the blankets, a bottle of whisky and this pillowcase. He must've taken them, come here and taken them.' David had thought it all out as they came across the fields, and the story came out now convincingly. Mr Reynolds nodded thoughtfully, but said nothing.

'And the plane?' he asked. 'No sign of that plane, I suppose.'

'We looked all around – there was nothing, not a sign.'

'Crashed into a bog,' Tucky blurted out, and David winced. They had agreed David would be the spokesman, that Tucky would keep quiet.

'How do you know that, my dear?' Mr Reynolds looked up sharply. 'He couldn't have told you, he doesn't speak English, does he?'

'He doesn't know, not really,' David said, willing Tucky to keep his mouth shut. 'Tucky's just guessing, that's all. Don't see what else could have happened though. We reckoned it must've crashed and then sank in a bog – that's what we thought anyway.'

'Ah,' Mr Reynolds nodded. 'There is that, I suppose. 'Tis a possibility, no doubt. And did you see any sign of anyone else up there, Germans, I mean? I was thinking that there's more than one man in a bomber crew, and it was a bomber wasn't it?' David nodded. The question was too close, and Mr Reynolds was talking strangely. He was suspicious; David was sure of it. 'Now there's as many as six or eight in one of their bombers, that's as far as I know, certainly more than one. I wonder what happened to the others?'

'Dead. They are all dead.' It was the German who spoke. David and Tucky looked at him in amazement.

'You speak English?' said Tucky.

'I speak English,' said the German, leaning back in the chair and shutting his eyes. 'I speak very good English.' And he did; there was an accent, but it was barely discernible.

'But I thought ...' Tucky remembered Mr Reynolds. 'That's the first time, Mr Reynolds, honest. He never said a word in English before, not a word.'

Mr Reynolds got up from the table and crouched down by the German's chair. 'The other men in the plane', he said, 'are they all dead?'

'All of them', the German said, opening his eyes and looking at Mr Reynolds. 'All of them, dead. My plane sunk under the ground; there was no time, I could not get them out.'

'And the blankets,' Mr Reynolds held up the one that was drying by the stove. 'Where did you get these from?' David and Tucky held their breath. David felt his nails biting into the palms of his hands, and his heart pounded in his ears.

'I was cold and I was hungry,' he spoke clearly. 'I stole them. This afternoon and yesterday afternoon I came here. The house was empty, there was no one here. I took blankets, eggs, whisky, anything I could find. I am sorry to steal from your house, but when a man is that hungry he will do anything. I had to eat.'

Mr Reynolds straightened up and put his hands on his hips. 'You were bombing Plymouth last week?'

'I can say nothing about that.' The German leant back and closed his eyes again.

'Well, my dears,' Mr Reynolds was smiling. 'I'm beginning to understand it now. Jip must've followed him back out on to the moor, and I sent you two out after Jip. Well, I'll be blowed. You wouldn't believe it, would you? I'll tell you something, they'll never believe it in the village, my dears, not till they see him anyway.' He looked at the German and back at the boys. 'Well, I'll be blowed. I'll be blowed.'

The German had cleared them on every count, and the boys could relax for the first time. David was tempted to catch his eye, to thank him, but he dared not take the risk. There was no point in spoiling it now, not just for a gesture. He felt Tucky smiling at him confidentially, and he ignored him. They were safe, but he felt no triumph, only relief.

CHAPTER 8

IT WAS NOT LONG BEFORE ANN CAME BACK with three soldiers and an officer from Okehampton. It was the same officer who had led the search the week before, the one with the mean face and thin moustache. David and Tucky grinned at him, but the officer ignored them, and looked frostily at Mr Reynolds when he said that two boys and a dog had succeeded when the army, the police and the Home Guard had failed. The boys enjoyed his obvious embarrassment.

The German remained silent as they took him away, but as he was leaving the cottage he turned and saluted, and the boys noticed his eyes were smiling as he did so. Then he was gone and the soldiers with him. Tucky begged to be allowed to go up to the village with the soldiers, but was told that the prisoner was being taken directly to Okehampton for questioning. There was to be no glory that night for Tucky.

But it came the next day. At school assembly Mr Cooper congratulated David and Tucky on their courage and tenacity, and the entire school clapped and cheered them. In the middle of morning lessons, two men from the local paper arrived to interview them and to take photographs. Tucky did most of the talking now, and David only interrupted him when he thought Tucky might be forgetting which story he was telling. Overnight the 'townies' had become local heroes, and the village crowed over their two boys who had surprised and captured a burly German pilot by themselves.

At home Mr Reynolds killed one of the old hens for a celebration supper, and Ann baked a rhubarb pie. It was the crest of the wave. But through it all, David could not help thinking about the German pilot upon the moor fighting his way through the wind and rain towards the coast, and the happier the evening became, the more he thought of the lies and trickery that had made it all possible.

Neither of them could sleep that night. Tucky, too, was thinking about the German out on the moor. 'How far d'you think he's got?'

'Dunno,' said David. 'Not far; he can't have got far.'

'He won't die, will he?' Tucky said. 'I don't want him to die, do you?'

'No,' David said. 'I don't, course I don't but I

don't want him to get away either.'

'Do you think anyone knows, Davey; about him, I mean?'

'Not now, not after what the German told Mr Reynolds.'

'I suppose he was trying to thank us, d'you think?'

'S'pose so.'

'Davey, I like being liked, don't you? Everyone liked us today, at school, in the village, here – everyone.'

'D'you think Ann and Mr Reynolds would like us if they ever found out?' David asked quietly.

'Doesn't matter, does it?' Tucky said, knocking his pillow into shape. 'They'll never find out, not now, not ever.'

'I hope not.' David squeezed his eyes tight shut. 'I hope not.'

It was nearly a week later and they were having their tea with Ann when Mr Reynolds came back from market with the newspaper. He spread it out on the kitchen table and stood back.

'There you are, my dears,' he said. 'Famous at last. You put the village on the front page of the *Western*

Morning News – 'tis the first time I've seen that.'

David and Tucky stared at their photograph. They were standing by the school gates. Tucky was grinning happily and giving the thumbs-up sign and he had his arm round David who was looking windswept and camera-shy.

The headline stood out in thick black lettering: 'Luftwaffe Pilot Captured by Village Boys.' And below was the story as Tucky had told it. They read it once and Tucky read it all through again, counting up the number of times his name was mentioned.

'They've cut it out and pinned it up on the wall in the village hall,' said Mr Reynolds. 'Like Ann and me, they're really proud of you.'

There was something in Mr Reynolds' voice that worried David. He glanced at Tucky to see if he had noticed it, but he hadn't. 'There's something else that might interest you,' he said from over his shoulders. 'Inside of the back page, let me turn it over.' He reached past them. 'There. There 'tis, where it says "German Airman Surrenders to Milkman". See it? You can read it if you'd like. 'Tis a good story, almost as good as yours.'

It was under the 'Late News' column down the side of the page, and it read: 'Milkman Harry Reddaway of

Belstone on his rounds in the village this morning was approached by a man claiming to be the pilot of a German bomber that crashed on the moor a fortnight ago. He said his plane had sunk in a bog and asked to be taken to the police. Mr Reddaway says the man was suffering from exposure. Police and army authorities believe he is from the same plane as the Luftwaffe pilot captured recently near Imberleigh, by two evacuee boys from London.'

David's mouth was dry when he'd finished reading it. He swallowed hard, and tried to speak normally. 'But he said they were all dead, didn't he? He said he was the only one left.'

' 'Tis natural enough, my dear. You'd hardly expect him to give his friend away, would you? 'Tis natural for a friend to protect a friend, isn't it? He was lying to us I'm afraid – about that anyway. No reason to lie about the rest, had he?'

There was no doubt now; at that moment both David and Tucky knew they were discovered. This time there was no quick answer, no way out. It was over. Only Ann looked puzzled. Mr Reynolds put his arm round her. ' 'Tis a little secret, Ann my dear, 'tis between Davey, Tucky and me, and that's an end of it. When they're ready no doubt they'll tell me why they did what they did, and then I can tell you, my dear.'

'He saved my life.' David felt his eyes warm with tears.

'We had to help them, just a little bit. He went in the river after Davey. We had to.' Tucky couldn't look them in the face.

Mr Reynolds nodded. 'I thought 'twould be something like that,' he said. 'They're fine boys, Ann. We often said that, haven't we, Ann? We often think that if we'd been blessed with children, we'd want to have them just like you two, and there's nothing'll change my mind.'

'You'll tell Ann?' David asked. 'You'll tell her everything?'

'Course I will, Davey, course I will, and then it'll be a secret between us all.'

'Was it wrong?' Tucky said quietly.

' 'Tis never wrong to do what you feel is right, Tucky,' said Mr Reynolds, ruffling his hair. 'Now, there's work to be done. There's a sheep or two gone out over the hedge on Back Meadow. Can you lend a hand, my dears?'

'Only one thing,' Mr Reynolds went on as they herded the sheep in through the gate, 'that bottle of whisky. I can forget the eggs, and Ann here, I expect she can forget the pie; but the whisky, that's a different matter. I won that in a raffle, that bottle, and I was going to make it last till the end of the war. You owe me one bottle of whisky – and when you're older and wiser and the war's all over, and past, perhaps you'd let me have it back, would you, my dears?'

And they did.

Today over thirty years later, Ann and Mr Reynolds have left the farm and moved up into a cottage in the village. Every year David and Tucky still come down to see them, and always when they come they bring Mr Reynolds his bottle of whisky. For Ann and Mr Reynolds it's the highlight of the year when their two 'children' from London, just the same but perhaps older and wiser, sit down in Ann's kitchen and remember the time when they helped Churchill win the war.

Waiting for Anya

CHAPTER 1

JO SHOULD HAVE KNOWN BETTER. AFTER ALL PAPA had told him often enough: 'Whittle a stick Jo, pick berries, eat, look for your eagle if you must,' he'd said, 'but do something. You sit doing nothing on a hillside in the morning sun with the tinkle of sheep bells all about you and you're bound to drop off. You've got to keep your eyes busy, Jo. If your eyes are busy then they won't let your brain go to sleep. And whatever you do, Jo, never lie down. Sit down but don't lie down.' Jo knew all that, but he'd been up since half past five that morning and milked a hundred sheep. He was tired, and anyway the sheep seemed settled enough grazing the pasture below him. Rouf lay beside him, his head on his paws, watching the sheep. Only his eyes moved.

Jo lay back on the rock and considered the lark rising above him and wondered why larks seem to perform when the sun shines. He could hear the church bells of Lescun in the distance but only faintly. Lescun, his village, his valley, where the people lived for their sheep and their cows. And they lived with them too. Half of each house was given over to the animals, a dairy on the ground floor, a hay loft above; and in front of every house was a walled yard that served as a permanent sheep fold.

For Jo the village was his whole world. He'd only been out of it a few times in all his twelve years, and one of those was to the railway station just two years before to see his father off to the war. They'd all gone, all the men who weren't too young and who weren't too old. It wouldn't take long to hammer the Boche and they'd be back home again. But when the news had come it had all been bad, so bad you couldn't believe it. There were rumours first of retreat and then of defeat, of French armies disintegrating, of English armies driven into the sea. Jo did not believe any of it at first, nor did anyone; but then one morning outside the Mairie he saw Grandpère crying openly in the street and he had to believe it. Then they heard that Jo's father was a prisoner-of-war in Germany and so were all the others who had gone from the village;

except Jean Marty, cousin Jean, who would never be coming back. Jo lay there and tried to picture Jean's face; he could not. He could remember his dry cough though and the way he would spring down a mountain like a deer. Only Hubert could run faster than Jean. Hubert Sarthol was the giant of the village. He had the mind of a child and could only speak a few recognisable words. The rest of his talk was a miscellany of grunting and groaning and squeaking but somehow he managed to make himself more or less understood. Jo remembered how Hubert had cried when they told him he couldn't join the army like the others. The bells of Lescun and the bells of the sheep blended in soporific harmony to lull him away into his dreams.

Rouf was the kind of dog that didn't need to bark too often. He was a massive white mountain dog, old and stiff in his legs but still top dog in the village and he knew it. He was barking now though, a gruff roar of a bark that woke Jo instantly. He sat up. The sheep were gone. Rouf roared again from somewhere behind him, from in among the trees. The sheep bells were loud with alarm, their cries shrill and strident. Jo was on his feet and whistling for Rouf to bring them back. They scattered out of the wood and came running and leaping down towards him. Jo thought it was a lone sheep at first that had got itself caught up on the edge of the wood, but then it barked as it backed away and became Rouf – Rouf rampant, hackles up, snarling; and there was blood on his side. Jo ran towards him calling him back and it was then that he saw the bear and stopped dead. As the bear came out into the sunlight she stood up, her nose lifted in the air. Rouf stayed his ground, his body shaking with fury as he barked.

The nearest Jo had ever been to a bear before was to the bearskin that hung on the wall in the café. Stood up as she was she was as tall as a full-grown man, her coat a creamy brown, her snout black. Jo could not find his voice to shout with, he could not find his legs to run with. He stood mesmerised, quite unable to take his eyes off the bear. A terrified ewe blundered into him and knocked him over. Then he was on his feet, and without even a look over his shoulder he was running down towards the village. He careered down the slopes, his arms flailing to keep his balance. Several times he tumbled and rolled and picked himself up again, but as he gathered speed his legs would run away with him once more. All it needed was a rock or a tussock of grass to send him sprawling once again. Bruised and bloodied he reached the track to the village and ran, legs pumping, head back, and shouting whenever he could find the breath to do it.

By the time he reached the village – and never had

it taken so long – he hadn't the breath to say more than one word, but one word was all he needed. 'Bear!' he cried and pointed back to the mountains, but he had to repeat it several times before they seemed to understand or perhaps before they would believe him. Then his mother had him by the shoulders and was trying to make herself heard through the hubbub of the crowd about them.

'Are you all right, Jo? Are you hurt?' she said.

'Rouf, Maman,' he gasped. 'There's blood all over him.'

'The sheep,' Grandpère shouted. 'What about the sheep?'

Jo shook his head. 'I don't know,' he said. 'I don't know.'

Monsieur Sarthol, Hubert's father and mayor of the village as long as Jo had been alive, was trying to organise loudly; but no one was paying him much attention. They had gone for their guns and for their dogs. Within minutes they were all gathered in the Square, some on horseback but most on foot. Those children that could be caught were shut indoors in the safekeeping of grandmothers, mothers or aunts; but many escaped their clutches and dived unseen into the narrow streets to join up with the hunting party as it left the village. A bear hunt was once in a lifetime and not to be missed. This was the stuff of legends and here was one in the making. Jo pleaded with Grandpère to be allowed to go but Grandpère could do nothing for him, Maman would have none of it. He was bleeding profusely from his nose and his knee, so despite all his objections he was bustled away into the house to have his wounds cleaned and bandaged. Christine, his small sister, gazed up at him with big eyes as Maman wiped away the blood.

'Where's the bear Jo?' Christine asked. 'Where's the bear?'

Maman kept saying he was as pale as a ghost and should go and lie down. He appealed one last time to Grandpère, but Grandpère ruffled his hair proudly, took his hunting rifle from the corner of the room and went out with everyone else to hunt the bear.

'Was it big, Jo?' said Christine tugging at his arm. She was full of questions. You could never ignore Christine or her questions – she wouldn't let you. 'Was it as big as Hubert?' And she held up her hands as high as she could.

'Bigger,' said Jo.

Bandaged like a wounded soldier he was taken up to his bedroom and tucked under the blankets. He stayed in bed only until Maman left the room, and then he sprang out of bed and ran to the window. He could see nothing but the narrow streets and the grey roofs of the village, and beyond the church-tower just a glimpse of the jagged mountain peaks still white in places with winter snow. The streets were empty of people, all except the priest, Father Lasalle, who was hurrying past, his hand on his hat to stop it blowing away.

All afternoon Jo watched as the clouds came down and began to swallow the valley. It was just after the church clock struck five that he heard a distant baying of dogs, and shortly after a volley of shots that echoed through the mountains and left a terrible silence hanging over the village.

He was down in the Square half an hour later with everyone else to watch the triumphant procession as it wound its way through the streets. Grandpère came first, Hubert gambolling alongside him.

'We got her,' Grandpère was shouting. 'We got her. Give us a hand here Hubert, give us a hand.' And they disappeared together into the café. They brought out two chairs each and set them down in front of the war memorial.

Limp in death, carried on two long poles by four men, the bear rocked into view, blood on her lolling tongue. She was laid out on the chairs, her legs hanging down on either side, her snout pressed up against the back of a chair. Jo was looking everywhere for Rouf but could not find him. He asked Grandpère if he had seen him but like everyone else Grandpère was too busy telling the story of the hunt or having his photograph taken. It was the grocer, Armand Jollet, who took pride of place in the photograph; it seemed he was the one who had actually shot the bear. He proclaimed this noisily, his round face red with pride and exhilaration. 'Two hundred metres away I was, and I hit him right between the eyes.'

'It's a she,' said Father Lasalle bending over the bear.

'What's the difference?' said Armand Jollet. 'He or she, that skin's worth a fortune.'

In the celebrations that followed the photograph, the war was suddenly forgotten. Even Marie, Cousin Jean's young widow, was laughing with them, swept along on a tide of communal joy and relief. Hubert clapped and cavorted about the place like a wild thing. He reared up like a bear and roared around the streets chasing screaming children and shouting, 'Baar! Baar!' Jo looked down at the bear and stroked her back. The fur was long and close and soft, the body still warm with life. Blood from the bear's nose dropped on to his shoe and he felt suddenly sick. He turned to run away but Monsieur Sarthol had his arm around his shoulders and was calling for silence.

'Here's the lad himself,' he said. 'Without Jo Lalande there'd be no bear. This is the first bear we have shot in Lescun for over twenty-five years.'

'Thirty,' said Father Lasalle.

The Mayor ignored him and went on. 'Lord knows how many of our sheep she'd have killed. We've a lot to thank him for.' Jo saw Maman's eyes smiling back at him in the front of the crowd but he could not smile back. The Mayor lifted his glass – most people seemed to have a glass in their hand by now. 'So, here's to Jo and here's to the bear, and down with the Boche.'

'Long live the bear,' someone shouted and the laughter that followed echoed in Jo's head. He could stand it no longer. He pulled away and ran, ignoring Maman's call to come back.

Until the Mayor's speech he had not thought about his part in it all. The she-bear was lying there dead, spread out on the chairs in the Square and he knew now it was all his doing. And perhaps Rouf was out there in the hills with his throat torn out, and none of it would have happened if he had not fallen asleep.

He ran all the way back along the track to the sheep pastures and up towards the trees. He stood there and called for Rouf again and again until his voice cracked, but only the crows answered him. He pushed the tears back out of his eyes and tried to calm himself, to remember the exact spot where he'd last seen Rouf. He called again, he whistled; but the clouds seemed to soak up the echoes. He looked up. There were no longer any mountains to be seen above the tree line, only a pall of thick mist. It was still now, not a whisper of wind. He could see where the sheep had been; there was wool caught on the bark of the trees, there were droppings here, footprints there. And then he saw the blood, Rouf's blood perhaps, a brown smattering on the root of a tree.

He could not be sure what it was that he was hearing, not at first. He thought perhaps it was the mewing of an invisible buzzard flying through the clouds but then he heard the sound again and knew it for what it was, the whining of a dog – high-pitched and distant but now quite unmistakable. He called and he climbed, it was too steep to run. He ducked under low-slung branches, he clambered over fallen trees calling all the while: 'I'm coming Rouf, I'm coming.'

The whining was punctuated now with a strange, intermittent growling, quite unlike anything he had heard before. He came upon Rouf sooner than he had expected. He spotted him through the trees sitting still as a rock, his head lowered as if he was pointing. He did not even turn round to look as Jo broke through into the clearing behind him. He seemed intent upon something in the mouth of a small cave. It was brown and it was small; and then it moved and became a bear cub. It was sitting in the shadows and waving one of its front paws at Rouf. Jo crouched down and put a hand on Rouf's neck. Rouf looked up at him whining with excitement. He licked his lips and resumed his focus on the bear cub, his body taut. The bear cub rocked back against the side of the cave, legs apart, and growled. Yet it was hardly a growl, more a bleat of hunger, a cry for help, a call for mother. 'They'll kill him, Rouf,' he whispered. 'If they find out about him they'll hunt him down and kill him, just like his mother.' Still looking at the bear he stroked Rouf's neck. It was matted and wet to the touch – like blood – but when he looked down at Rouf there wasn't a mark on him.

Suddenly Rouf was on his feet, he swung round, hackles up, a rumbling growl in his throat. Jo turned. There was a man standing under the trees at the edge of the clearing. He wore a dirty black coat, a battered hat on his head. They looked at each other. Rouf stopped growling and his tail began to wag.

'Only me again,' said the man coming out of the trees towards them. Even with his hat he was a short man and as he came closer Jo saw that he had the gaunt, grey look of old men, yet his beard was rust red with not a fleck of white in it. There was a wine bottle in one hand and a stick in the other.

'Milk,' he said holding out the bottle. Rouf sniffed at it and the man laughed. 'Not for you,' he said and he patted Rouf on the head. 'For the little fellow. Starving he is. Perhaps you'd hold my stick for me,' he said. 'We don't want to frighten him do we?' He gave his hat to Jo as well and took off his coat. 'I saw the whole thing, you know. I saw you running off too. Your dog is he?' Jo nodded. 'Fights like a tiger doesn't he? Bears like that can knock your head off you know. One swipe of the paw that's all it takes. He was lucky. She tore his ear a bit, a lot of blood; but we soon cleaned you up didn't we old son? Right as rain he is now.' He bent down and poured some milk on to a rock. 'Now, let's see if we can get this little fellow to take a drink.' He backed away a few paces and knelt down. 'He'll smell it soon, you'll see. Give him time and he won't be able to resist it.' He sat back on his heels.

The cub ventured out of the shadows of the cave, lifting his nose and sniffing the air as he came. 'Come on, come on little fellow,' said the man, 'we won't hurt you.' And he reached out very slowly and poured out some more milk but closer to the bear cub this time. 'She could've got away you know.'

'Who?' said Jo.

'The bear, the mother bear. I've been thinking

about it. She was leading them away from her cub. Deliberate it was, I'm sure of it. And what's more she led them a fair old dance I can tell you. Did you see the hunt?' Jo shook his head. 'Right away down the valley she took them, I saw it all – well most of it anyway. Course I couldn't know why she was doing that, not at the time; and then I was on my way back home through the woods and there was this little fellow, and your dog just sitting here watching him. Covered in blood he was. Once I'd cleaned him up I went back home for some milk – the only thing I could think of. There you are, he's coming for it now.' The cub came forward tentatively, touched the milk with his paw, smelt it, licked it to taste and then began to lap noisily. Suddenly the man's free arm shot out and scooped the cub on to his lap. There was a flurry of paws and a furious scratching and yowling until all the flailing arms and legs were trapped. His whole head was white with milk by now but the end of the bottle was in his mouth and he was sucking in deeply. The man looked up at Jo and smiled. He had milk all over his beard and was licking his lips. 'Got him,' he said and he chuckled until he laughed. The cub still clung to the bottle when it was empty and would not let go.

'He'll die out here on his own won't he?' said Jo.

'No he won't, not if we don't let him,' said the

man and he tickled the cub under his chin. 'Someone's going to have to look after him.'

'I can't,' said Jo. 'They'd kill him. If I took him home they'd kill him, I know they would.' He touched the pad of the cub's paw, it was harder than he'd expected. The man thought for a while nodding slowly.

'Well then, I'll have to do it, won't I?' he said. 'Won't be long, only a month or two at the most I should think and then he'll be able to cope on his own. I've got nothing much else to do with myself, not at the moment.' For just a moment as he caught his eye Jo thought he recognised the man from somewhere before but he could not think where. Yet he was sure he knew everyone who lived in the valley – not by name necessarily, but by place or by face. 'You don't know who I am do you?' said the man. It was as if he could read Jo's thoughts. Jo shook his head. 'Well that makes us even doesn't it, because I don't know you either. Maybe it's better it stays that way. You've got to promise me never to say a word, you understand?' There was a new urgency in his voice. 'There was no cub, you never met me, you never even saw me. None of this ever happened.' He reached out and gripped Jo's arm tightly. 'You have to promise me. Not a word to anyone – not your father, not your mother, not your best friend, no-one, not ever.'

'All right,' said Jo who was becoming alarmed. He felt the grip on his arm relax.

'Good boy, good boy,' he said and patted Jo's arm.

The man looked up. The mist was filtering down through the treetops above them. 'I'd better get back,' he said. 'I don't want to get caught out in this, I'll never find my way home.'

Once he was on his feet Jo gave him his hat and his stick. 'Now you hang on to that dog of yours,' he said. 'I don't want him following me home. Where one goes others can follow, if you understand my meaning.' Jo wasn't sure he did. The cub clambered up his shoulder and put an arm around his neck. 'Seems to like me, doesn't he?' said the man. He turned to go and then stopped. 'And don't you go blaming yourself for what happened this afternoon. You had your job to do, and that old mother bear she had hers to do and that's all there is to it. Besides,' and he smiled broadly as the cub snuffled in his ear, 'besides, if none of it had happened, we'd never have met would we?'

'We haven't met,' said Jo catching Rouf by the scruff of his neck as he made to follow them. The man laughed.

'Nor we have,' he said. 'Nor we have. And if we haven't met we can't say goodbye can we?' And he turned, waved his stick above his head and walked away into the trees, the cub's chin resting on his shoulder. The eyes that looked back at Jo were two little moons of milk.

CHAPTER 2

JO STOOD IN THE CLEARING AND LISTENED UNTIL he could no longer hear the man's footsteps. The whole day had been like a bad dream that had turned suddenly and intensely intriguing – a dream he wanted to cling to. He knew if he walked away now he might never see the man or the bear cub again. He had to find out who he was and where he was going. He knew he shouldn't but he had to follow him all the same.

Rouf did not have to be asked to follow the scent. He simply walked away into the trees and Jo went after him. From time to time he stopped to listen, but all he heard was Rouf's purposeful panting ahead of him and the soft whisper of the mist falling through the trees. After a while he began to wonder if Rouf's nose was failing him because they were following no track through the forest. Jo found himself sometimes climbing steeply and then scrambling downwards again clutching at treetrunks to keep himself upright. They seemed to be going back on themselves, almost round in circles at one point; but Rouf seemed sure enough of himself, plodding on resolutely until they broke out of the trees. Jo found himself looking down on the slate roofs of a farmstead.

He recognised at once where they were although he had never been near the place nor seen it from quite his direction. It was Widow Horcada's farm. She lived alone up in the hills and kept herself to herself. She seemed to like it that way. She must have had a husband once but Jo had never known him and no one ever spoke of him. So far as anyone could tell she lived off her pigs that wandered everywhere – much to everyone's annoyance – off one cow and off her honey; you could find her beehives ranged all along the hillside above the village. There was a line of them below him now, just a few metres away, but no bees that Jo could see. Jo had no desire to go any closer, and it wasn't because he was afraid of bees.

Widow Horcada was not much liked in the village – 'sinister' Maman always called her – although Grand-père always defended her stoutly. The children in the village called her 'The Black Widow', and not just on account of the long black shawl she always wore over her head. Like every child in the village Jo had been mauled more than once by her sharp tongue. She made no secret of the fact that she did not like children, boys in particular. She was a person to avoid. He would go no further. But before Jo could grab him, Rouf was making his way past the beehives and down towards the buildings. Jo followed, whispering as loud as he dared for Rouf to stop. But Rouf did not stop.

There was a cow grazing in the small paddock below the house, her bell sounded as she pulled at the grass and looked up. The walled farmyard was full of snuffling, snorting pigs and that was clearly too much for Rouf – he did not like pigs, not one bit. He sat down outside the wall and waited for Jo. A light was on in the house and there were dark figures moving about in the downstairs room. There were voices coming from inside, raised voices; but he was too far away to hear what they were saying. One thing was certain though; one of the voices belonged to the man he had been following.

Jo thought of jumping the wall and running low across the yard towards the window but the boar was wandering towards him with menace in his eyes; so Jo went around the back. There was only one window, and to reach it he would have to climb up a stack of wood that was piled high against the wall. He climbed carefully until he could pull himself up and peer over the windowsill.

There were two people in the room. The man was bent over the sink splashing water over his face and Widow Horcada sat in a chair by the stove knitting feverishly. She was shaking her head and muttering something that Jo couldn't hear. The man was wiping his face with a towel and talking through it at the same time.

'Don't you go worrying yourself about the boy,' he said. 'He doesn't know who I am, what I am or where I live. We'll be all right.' He dropped the towel over the back of a chair and sat down at the table feeling his beard. 'Worst thing about a beard,' he said, 'it never dries properly.' And at that moment Jo remembered where he'd seen the man before.

It was the last summer before Papa had gone off to the war and he'd been up in the high mountain pastures with Papa, the first time he'd been allowed to go. Three long months they had spent up there together in the hut, milking the sheep every morning making the cheese, then milking the sheep again in the evening. It had been a summer of hard work and soaring happiness – a summer alone with Papa, a summer living close to the eagles. Most people walking in the mountains passed by with a 'Good morning', or perhaps a request to drink at the spring but only two had ever come into the hut. They had appeared early one morning, a man with a red beard, a little girl clutching his hand. She'd have been five or six years old maybe with red hair like his. They had stayed until noon watching the sheep being milked and the cheese being made. They sat side by side and silent on Papa's bed and watched fascinated as the rennet was poured in, as they heated and stirred the milk in the cauldrons, as Papa gathered the curd in his hands and squeezed out the whey. Jo remembered their silence and the intense seriousness on the little girl's face. They asked the way up to the Spanish border and went off. It was raining when they came back later that afternoon. They brought with them a bunch of flowers, pinks they were and wild pansies. Jo could see them now in her hand. 'From Spain to you,' said the little girl, ushered forward by her father; and the man with the beard told them how they had walked to the top of the mountain and looked into Spain and how their legs ached. Papa had given them towels to dry themselves off. 'Never grow a beard young man,' the man had told him as he wiped his face. 'You can never get it dry.' Jo remembered Papa thanking them rather awkwardly and saying that no one had ever given him flowers before. They were already leaving before they introduced themselves. 'I'm Madame Horcada's son-in-law,' he said shaking Papa's hand, 'and this is my daughter, Anya.'

Watching them walk away down the mountain Papa had told him the story of Widow Horcada's daughter – Florence she was called. Jo thought he remembered seeing her in church once when he was little but he couldn't be sure. She'd gone off to Paris Papa told him, run off some said, and got herself married. No one knew who to because she'd never brought him back to Lescun. 'So that was the husband,' said Papa. 'Well I never.'

'Where's Widow Horcada's daughter?' Jo had asked.

'Dead,' said Papa. 'Dead in childbirth I heard, and that must be the child. Poor little mite.' Papa had kept the dead flowers all summer long on the shelf above his bed but they never spoke of the visitors again.

'Foolhardy,' said Widow Horcada, putting the knitting down on her lap. 'Plain foolhardy, that's what it was. I just don't understand what came over you, Benjamin. Stay as long as it takes I said. Do what you have to do and I'll help you all I can. We agreed, didn't we? You promised you'd go out only at night. You promised me, didn't you? And what do you do? You go out for a walk in broad daylight. A walk! And what do you bring back? Not berries, not herbs, not mushrooms, but an orphan bear cub. I ask you Benjamin, haven't we got troubles enough?' She leaned forward in her chair, her crooked finger pointing. 'And that boy you met, what happens now, eh? You tell me that. What happens when he runs home and tells them all down in the village? Well, I'll tell you. Someone will put two and two together and they'll know the old widow's son-in-law is back. They don't forget a face you know, especially not your face. They may be country folk, Benjamin, but they're not stupid.'

The man left the table and crouched down in front of her taking both her hands in his. 'Believe me, Grandmère,' he said, 'the boy won't say anything. I can always tell an honest face.' He smiled up at her. 'I know I'm not all you wanted in a son-in-law but I tell you true, you're all I could ever have wanted in a mother-in-law.'

'Go on with you,' she said trying to push him away, but he held on to her hands.

'No I mean it. You're brave and you're good and I couldn't have done any of it without you. You know that.'

'I don't know anything,' she said, 'not any more I don't. Maybe you're right about that boy, maybe he won't say anything. Let's just pray to God you're right.'

'Your God or mine?' said the man laughing.

'Why not both?' the widow said, 'just in case one of us is barking up the wrong tree.' She reached out and touched his face. 'You're all I've got left now Benjamin, you and little Anya – if she's still alive.'

'Course she is,' said the man. 'How many times do I have to tell you?'

'You've been telling me for two years now,' said the widow.

'Two years, ten years,' he said, 'however long it takes. She'll come. And when she does we'll be waiting for her just like I promised her. She knows where to come and she'll be here, you'll see. She could walk in here tonight.'

Widow Horcada sighed and looked up at the window. 'It's getting dark,' she said, starting up from her chair, 'I'd better see to the animals.' And then she saw him.

Jo felt the logs give under his feet. He tried to hold on to the window ledge but his fingers were cold and would not grip as they should. For a fleeting moment he saw their faces staring up at him and then he was falling in an avalanche of logs that sent him tumbling down on to the cobbled stone of the yard. He kicked frantically and pushed the logs away. Then he was on his feet and running before he heard the back door open. He dared not turn round and look. For the second time that day Jo found himself running down the slopes, but this time there was a misty darkness to hide him and he could afford to stop from time to time to regain his breath. Rouf ran on ahead of him and was waiting for him on his sack by the front doorstep. Jo had to step over him to open the door. Rouf yawned hugely and put his head on his paws. Clearly for him it had been no more than an ordinary day.

For some weeks after this the village was diverted, its spirits lifted by stories of the great bear hunt, stories that eclipsed even the grim news of the war, of more German victories everywhere. They heard about the world outside through newspapers that few people believed because they were controlled by the Germans, but also through Radio London and what you heard there had to be believed. There was no consolation to be gleaned from either source, so they talked of the bear hunt to forget the war and for a time they could do so.

At school Jo had become quite the hero and that was not entirely to his liking. If Jo had learned one lesson at school it was that it was better to keep a low profile – that way you kept out of trouble. But now he was thrust suddenly into the limelight. He had admirers and therefore enemies too. Even his best friend, Laurent, seemed to look at him differently. Only Monsieur Audap, his teacher, was quite unimpressed by the whole thing. Strict as he was, severe even at times, Monsieur Audap was scrupulously fair, and was liked and respected for it. A retiring man, he said very little, but what he did say was always worth listening to.

The day after Armand Jollet put up the bearskin on the wall of his grocer's shop for all the world to admire, Monsieur Audap spent the entire morning telling the children all about the mountain bears, about where they lived and how they lived. After hibernation, he said, in the Spring when their body fat was low and they had young to feed, then they would dare anything to find food enough to provide for themselves and for their cubs. Bears, he said, never came close to people unless they had to. They knew of their cruelty, of their voracious appetite for killing and of their greed. Bears, he said, were neither stupid nor suicidal. This one must have been starving to have risked such an attack. Almost certainly, said Monsieur Audap, she had cubs to feed – usually there were two, maybe just one. They'd be dead by now, of course. They needed their mother's milk for at least three or four months. Jo looked down at his desk so that his eyes would not betray him.

As time passed though the bear talk both in and out of school became less frequent and less triumphalist; and once again news of the war, of unending, depressing defeats began to preoccupy the village. But to many of the children, to Jo too, the war was still an unreal thing. In over two years of war they had not seen a single German soldier, no planes, no tanks, nothing. The war was in the talk and they heard plenty of that; and talk almost always meant argument. What should they do? Should they save what could be saved? Should they accept the finality of defeat and join Maréchal Pétain, or should they fight on with the English and join the French colonel, whose name Jo could never remember but who had broadcast from London that the war was not over, that the Germans could be beaten, must be beaten and would be beaten? And all the while they waited for the prisoners-of-war to come home and they didn't. They waited for the Germans to come and they didn't.

'I just want it over with, Jo,' Maman said. 'I want your father home. I don't care what it takes. I want it like it was before.' And although Grandpère did not often argue with her openly, Jo knew what he thought. 'That Colonel in London, that De Gaulle, he's our only hope I tell you,' Grandpère had told him. 'Him and the

English. I don't like the English, never have done, but at least they're fighting the Germans and anyone who is fighting them is a friend of France, that's how I see it. And I should know, Jo, I fought them before, remember? We beat them then and we'll beat them again. We've got to. There'll be nothing left for you or for any of us if we don't.' What Jo thought about the war and about the occupation seemed to depend on whether he had just talked to Maman or to Grandpère: he could never make up his mind.

Jo thought often of Papa as he sat on his rock watching the sheep. He had missed him at first, the loudness of him about the house and the smell of him when he came in from work; but now as time passed he was enjoying his new role as the man about the house. He enjoyed sitting in Papa's chair at the kitchen table and doing Papa's work about the farm. But whether it was the war or whether it was Papa competing for his thoughts, Jo's mind was always drawn back to the bear cub and the man he'd met in the woods on the day of the bear hunt. He had to know who he was, what he was hiding from and why he was waiting for Anya. Every passing day only intensified his longing to go back up to the Widow Horcada's farm to find out what was going on and to see the bear cub again. But there was always work to be done, farm work, school work. It was difficult to get away – that was what he told himself anyway.

Grandpère took the sheep to the high pastures that summer. Jo was still too young, Maman said, to do it on his own and she didn't want him missing any more school. 'You only get your learning once,' she said, and besides she needed him at home – there was the bracken to cut and to turn, or the hay to make; and at weekends there were the supplies to be taken up to Grandpère in the mountains and the cheeses brought back to be salted, stored and sold. The work was long and hard, but if Jo was honest with himself – and as time passed he had to be – he knew the work was an excuse. The fact was that he could not summon up the courage to go back to Widow Horcada's farm. Every time he had seen her coming he'd hidden from her; and the one time he couldn't avoid her, when she'd come into the grocer's shop, he'd run out without buying what he went in there for. He hadn't even dared to look her in the eye to see if she recognised him as the boy peering in through her window that evening.

Time and again he had looked up the hillside towards her farmhouse and had seen the Widow Horcada out in her fields, making her hay, milking her cow or driving her pigs, but there'd been no sign of anyone else. He was beginning to think he had imagined the whole thing.

Then one blustery Autumn day, after the sheep had come down from the pastures and he was spreading out the bracken for their bedding in the barn, he saw Widow Horcada scurrying past, black scarf over her head, flowers in her hand. He knew she'd be making for the churchyard to put flowers on her husband's grave. She'd stop to do her shopping on the way back, she always did. Jo knew he had a clear half hour to get up there and back: he could do it if he hurried. She'd never see him, not if he was careful. Rouf tried to come with him as he always did. He shut him in the barn and shouted to Maman that he wouldn't be long.

He kept under the cover of the trees as long as he could. From there he could see without being seen. Her pigs were foraging in the field below the house and the cow was lying curled asleep in the middle of them. There was no one about. He threw caution to the wind because he had to – there was no time for anything else. He hared across the field until he reached the safety of the barn wall where he knew he could not be seen from the house. He ran around the back of the barn and into the courtyard behind. There was no sound except for the contented grunting of rooting pigs. He was creeping past the barn door when he heard something shuffling around inside. The bear cub, it must be the bear cub.

He looked about him and then opened the door slowly. Like all the barns it was long and low and dark, with bracken on the floor and hay in the wooden rack that ran the length of the wall. But there was no bear cub, and no other animals either. Yet he was sure he'd heard something, quite sure. He pushed the door wide open so as to throw as much light as possible down the barn. There was one small dirty window at the far end, and the shutters were banging open and shut, first one and then the other. Jo peered into the darkness. He would go no further. He could see well enough from the doorway. He was turning to go when he trod on something. He bent down and picked up a shoe, a child's shoe. The strap was broken. He thought little of it at first. He would have dropped it and left had he not heard the breathing – a regular wheezing breathing.

It came quite definitely from the hayrack about halfway down the barn. Jo took a few steps towards it and the breathing stopped. He thought of the bear cub and of the hibernation Monsieur Audap had told them about, but he thought that it couldn't be the bear cub because it wasn't winter yet and anyway a bear cub would hardly be sleeping in a hayrack – but then perhaps it would. He took a few more tentative steps forward and peered into the hay. The breathing began again a little further on and quite suddenly he found himself not looking at hay at all but at two eyes that stared back at him unblinking and terrified. Jo could do nothing for a moment but stare back into them. They were not the eyes of a bear for the face that went with them was pale and thin under a fringe of dark hair.

Jo backed away slowly, swallowing his fear. He had the presence of mind to close the door quietly and it was just as well he did for across the yard Widow Horcada was bent over, holding a bucket under an outdoor tap. She had her back to him and was humming quietly to herself. For a few moments he stood looking at her disbelieving. How could she be back so soon? It wasn't possible. Yet there she was in front of him. She had only to turn round. It was just a few steps to the corner of the barn and safety. He'd make it if he could move silently. Without taking his eyes off her he began to inch his way along the wall.

He knew he should have looked where he was going. He told himself so as the fork he blundered into clattered to the ground. Jo looked at the Widow Horcada, the bucket fell out of her hand as the black shawl swung round. Jo dropped the shoe, stumbled over the fork and ran and ran. He rounded the corner of the barn, but there he was stopped in his tracks, for up the hill, a large basket in one hand, a stick in the other, came Widow Horcada. She looked up, saw him and shouted at him. He could not hear what she was saying. Jo turned again and ran back into the yard – it was the only way he could go. She was there too and coming towards him. He looked now from one to the other. Fear crept up his spine like a warm cat and he felt the hair rise on the back of his neck. Never in all his life had he felt like screaming until this moment. He wanted to but he could not. And then one of them spoke, the one striding across the yard towards him.

'It's me.' It was a man's voice. 'It's me.' And he pulled the shawl off his head. The red beard was longer than Jo remembered but it was the same man. 'Don't you remember me?' he said.

CHAPTER 3

JO HAD NOWHERE TO RUN TO EVEN IF HE'D wanted to and he wasn't sure now that he did. The man stooped to pick up the shoe.

'And where did you find this then?' he asked.

'In the barn,' said Jo. 'I was only looking. I thought you might have the bear cub in there.' The man wiped the shoe on the end of the shawl. There were footsteps coming into the yard behind him. Jo turned. The Black Widow stood there breathing hard, resting her weight on her stick. The man went over to her and took the basket.

'It's all right Grandmère,' he said putting an arm around her. 'It's that boy, the same boy.' Widow Horcada limped across the yard towards him. It was all

Jo could do not to back away. She looked at him long and hard.

'Well, well,' she said, 'so it was you. I thought as much. I wasn't sure, not until you pushed past me in the shop the other day. I knew then all right. You shouldn't go peeking through other people's windows.' She caught sight of the shoe in the man's hand. 'So he knows then,' she said.

'He's been in the barn,' he said.

'Has he indeed?' said the Widow. 'And what did you find in there boy?'

There was no point in futile protestations and denials but Jo tried them anyway. 'I don't know what you mean,' he said feebly.

She stabbed her stick into the ground by his foot. 'Besides the shoe,' she said, 'did you see anything else in there? Well, did you?' Jo looked down to avoid her eyes. 'I don't like a child that won't look me in the eye,' she said and she lifted his chin until he had to look at her. Jo had never looked at her this closely and he was surprised by what he saw. It was not the cruel face he had always supposed but leathery and lined with age and work.

'Yes, I did,' Jo said. She released his chin.

'And do you always speak the truth?' she asked quietly.

Jo shook his head. 'No,' he said and her face cracked into a sudden smile.

'Seems you were right then, Benjamin. A rare thing, an honest boy. Inside,' she said, 'bring him inside,' and she walked away towards the door. 'Boys like honey,' she said. 'We'll give him some honey.' And she disappeared inside the house.

Jo was reluctant to follow. The man put a hand on his shoulder. 'Have you still got him?' Jo asked. 'The bear cub, have you still got him?'

The man shook his head. 'Not any more. A month after we found him, just as soon as I thought he could fend for himself, I took him high up into the mountains and left him but he's been coming back from time to time. I think maybe he thinks of me as his mother, either that or he just doesn't like being on his own. Come on.'

Widow Horcada was putting a plate of honeycomb out on the table. Suddenly the old lady leaned forward and had to hold on to the table to steady herself. The man was by her side at once and helped her to her chair.

'You've been overdoing it again,' he said. 'I've told you haven't I?'

'Don't fuss,' she said, pushing him away. 'Don't fuss me. I'll be all right. Sit down boy, sit down over there in the light, I want to be able to see your face.' Jo sat down at the table. 'Eat up, boy, eat up.' She had a strange habit of wrinkling her nose and sniffing and Jo found it difficult not to stare at her. He cut out a corner of the honeycomb and spread it on the bread. The man was hanging the big shawl on the back of the door.

'I know your father,' said Widow Horcada, not taking her eyes off his face. 'Prisoner-of-war isn't he?' Jo nodded. 'I knew your grandfather better though. I told you about him didn't I Benjamin?' Benjamin nodded and she turned back to Jo. 'I nearly married him once. Did he ever tell you that, boy? Sweethearts we were.' She sighed and sat back in her chair. 'Ah well, we both went our separate ways for better or for worse. You're not eating, boy.' Jo took another mouth ful. 'Jo Lalande he's called, aren't you, boy? And you know who I am don't you?' Jo nodded. 'This is Benjamin, my son-in-law, but then of course you've met him before, haven't you?' She paused for a moment, her searching eyes still fixed on Jo. She blew her nose and tucked her handkerchief into her sleeve. 'Well,' she said. 'I suppose he'll have to be told. Nothing else for it is there? But I don't like it. I don't like it one bit.'

'It'll be all right,' said Benjamin. He was standing behind her now and looking down at Jo. 'What he doesn't know already – and he knows plenty – he's guessed at, and guessing is a lot more dangerous than knowing. And we know we can trust him. After all he's known about us for months now, and he's not said a word. If he had then we'd have known about it you can be sure of that. We'd have had the police knocking on the door in the middle of the night by now. No, we don't need to worry about him. We can trust him.'

'Let's hope so,' said the Widow wearily. 'Let's hope so.'

Benjamin came and sat down opposite Jo at the table. 'It's difficult to know where to start, Jo,' he said, 'but since I'm the cause of all the trouble I'll start with me. I'm a Jew,' he said. 'D'you know what that is?'

'They're in the Bible aren't they?' said Jo.

Benjamin shook his head and laughed. 'Yes,' he said. 'We're in the Bible and there's plenty of people think that's where we should've stayed.' He looked down at his hands and picked at the corner of his thumb nail. 'It was all rumours at first,' he went on, 'rumours you couldn't believe, rumours you didn't want to believe. But bit by bit the rumours became facts, facts that had to be believed. They began on their own Jews, in Germany. First they took away their work, then their property; and they made them wear yellow stars on their coats. Then they started rounding them up and sending them off to the camps. We knew it was happening but we thought we were safe enough in Paris, me and little Anya – Anya, she's my daughter. But of course we weren't. They invaded France and Paris fell. There was only one place left we could go. We came here for a holiday a few years back, Anya and me, to see where her mother was brought up, to see Grandmère. The happiest time of our lives it was too. So when the invasion came we decided to come back here.'

'Best place too, long as you're sensible,' said the Widow Horcada pointedly. 'Safe as houses and you can be over the border in five hours.'

'I walked it once,' said Benjamin, 'with Anya.'

'I know,' said Jo. 'You picked flowers for my father.'

Benjamin frowned for a moment and then his eyes brightened suddenly. 'So it was you. You were the boy. You remember I told you, Grandmère, that day that we watched the shepherd making cheese. He was your father?' Jo nodded. 'And you were the little boy, weren't you? Well, well, it's a small world.' The light left his eyes as quickly as it had come. 'We left Paris together, Anya and me. Trouble was everyone was doing the same thing and the roads were jammed with cars and carts and lorries and people – thousands of people, everyone trying to get away. They machine-gunned us from the air whenever they felt like it and when the planes came we all scattered. After they'd gone it was always difficult to find each other again; so we made an agreement, Anya and me, that if we were separated we would find our way back here, to Grandmère's house at Lescun, we would wait for each other and then we could escape together into Spain. We said we'd wait, we promised each other.' His voice choked, and it was a moment or two before he went on. 'And that's just how it happened. One evening – just outside Poitiers it was – the planes came and strafed us and we all ran for shelter into the forest. When they'd gone I looked everywhere for her. All night I looked for her, all next day and the day after, but I couldn't find her. So that's why I'm here and that's why I'll be staying till Anya comes.'

'But what about her, in there,' said Jo, 'in the barn?'

'She's called Léah,' said Benjamin. 'Same age to the month as Anya. She comes from Poland just like my family did many years ago. We've got two more coming soon.'

'Two more?'

'Children,' said Widow Horcada sniffing. 'Jewish children. He collects them, don't you Benjamin?' Benjamin said nothing. 'They get passed down all through France and when they get here he keeps them for a week maybe, sometimes longer, till they're strong enough for the journey; and then he takes them over the mountains into Spain and to safety.'

'And so many of them,' said Benjamin, 'so many are just like Léah. She had a big family, eight children there were. She's the oldest and she's the last. She was lucky; she was out when the soldiers came to the house. She watched her family being taken away, and she's been on the run ever since. But she got here, and that's why we'll never give up hope. If Léah can get here all the way from Poland then so can Anya. One day Anya will be one of these children and we'll be waiting for her.'

'That shawl you were wearing,' said Jo.

Ben was smiling again. 'Oh that. That was your idea, wasn't it Grandmère? Do you know, Jo, I never once went out of this house for two years unless it was to take the children over the mountains and then it was always in the dark. Then the first time I venture out for a walk in the daytime I bump into you, and I bring home a bear cub. She wasn't too pleased about that. She lets me out by day now, but only if I stay close to the house and only if I dress up to look like her. She's a terrible tyrant is my mother-in-law.'

'Stuff and nonsense,' she said.

At that moment they all heard something at the

door. They saw the handle turn. It opened slowly, squeaking on its hinges, and a small face peered round. It was the girl from the barn. Benjamin ran across the room and pulled her inside. Then he looked out of the door and shut it, leaning back against it and breathing hard. 'It's all right,' he said. When he spoke again it was in a language Jo could not understand. He crouched down, holding the girl by her shoulders, and he was clearly angry with her. But the girl was not listening to him. Her eyes were fixed on the honey on the table beside Jo. She walked towards it now as if she was in a trance. She pulled the plate towards her, dug her finger into the honeycomb and scooped it into her mouth.

'She eats all the time,' said Widow Horcada. 'It's like she's never eaten before.'

The girl saw her shoe on the table and took it. She dropped it on to the floor and stepped into it without looking down. Jo looked at her as she ate. Her face was impassive except for her eyes that flitted nervously around the room. There was hay in her hair and on her coat. Benjamin beckoned her over and she went slowly towards him. When she sat on his lap she looked back at Jo, sucking her finger. And then Benjamin began to sing softly in the girl's ear. She put her hand up and curled her fingers in his beard. It was a song Jo had never heard before and in a strange language. He sang in a deep resonant voice that filled the room. He rocked her back and forth as he sang and gradually she settled back against his shoulder and hummed with him. All the while she never stopped looking at Jo. She was asleep in a few minutes, her finger in her mouth.

'I've told you Benjamin, I've told you,' Widow Horcada was whispering, 'they must stay in the barn. You must tell her, Benjamin. We can't have them wandering around. They must stay where they're told.'

'You're right,' said Benjamin, 'but I have told her, again and again. She's lonely in there, Grandmère. When the others come it'll be better. She'll have friends then and she'll stay put.'

'All right,' said the Widow. 'But just you make sure she does. Just a glimpse of one of those children of yours and we're done for – you know that don't you?'

'I know,' said Benjamin. 'I know.'

She turned to Jo. 'And you'd best be off home.' As Jo got up she reached out and grabbed his wrist. 'I was thinking,' she said, drawing him towards her. 'I was thinking of swearing you to secrecy.' She patted a book on the table beside her. 'On the Bible. Do I need to?'

'No,' said Jo.

'Off you go then,' said Widow Horcada, 'and if you see me down in the village behave like they all do, all except Hubert. He's the only one that smiles at me, but then he smiles at everyone doesn't he? Don't even look at me. I'm still the Black Widow, remember?' Jo turned to go. 'And another thing, boy; stay away from here. Don't come back. We don't want any comings and goings. I want them to forget I'm here. It's safer that way. You understand?'

'Yes,' said Jo.

She waved him away. 'Off home with you now.'

Jo was so occupied with his thoughts as he made his way home that he took no notice at all of the empty, silent streets; but as he reached the Square his thoughts were rudely interrupted. The whole village was there standing hushed and unmoving, like mourners at a funeral. Jo eased his way through the crowd so that he could see what was going on. An armoured truck stood in the centre of the Square with four soldiers in black uniforms and shining helmets sitting erect in the back of it. Beside it Monsieur Sarthol was talking earnestly to a tall German officer who appeared not to be listening. '*Ja, ja,*' he said dismissively. '*Ja, ja,*' and he turned to the soldier beside him and nodded. The soldier walked towards the Mairie, the crowd parting in front of him. He leaned his rifle against the wall and pinned up a poster. Jo could see two faces on it and some writing below. The officer clicked his heels, saluted the Mayor and got back into the truck.

Hubert was standing next to Grandpère, towering over him. There was naked anger on his face. Jo knew he was going to do something; he could feel it coming. He did not have long to wait. Hubert barged his way through the crowd and walked straight towards the German officer. He was carrying a short stick in his hand. The soldier walking back from the Mairie, saw Hubert and readied his rifle. The officer shouted to him and held up his hand. Hubert kept walking until he was about a metre away from the officer. Slowly and deliberately he raised his stick to his shoulder and pointed it at his face. 'Bang,' he said softly. 'Bang, bang, bang.' The Mayor was rushing forward. He grabbed Hubert by the arm and pulled him back.

'He's my son,' he said. 'He doesn't mean anything. It's just his little joke. He's not quite right in the head, you understand. A bit simple. He won't hurt you.' The officer nodded curtly and motioned the soldier to get in.

Throughout this the four soldiers in the truck had sat impassive, their rifles between their knees. Jo stared at them and despite himself he could not but admire them. They were undeniably splendid in their immaculate uniforms. These were the black knights who had conquered wherever they went. He was staring at one of them in particular when the helmet turned, glinting in the sun, and Jo found his gaze suddenly returned. The eyes that held his were blue and cold and they chilled Jo to the heart. He looked away quickly. The truck started up, circled the Square and was gone.

Everyone crowded towards the poster, but Monsieur Sarthol stepped in front of it and held up his hand.

'All in good time,' he shouted. 'All in good time. First you must hear what he told me.' People still weren't listening and he raised his voice. 'You've got to listen to me. You've got to hear it.' They quietened enough for him to go on. 'He came to remind us that all of France is now occupied, that we are in a forbidden zone, that no one goes in or out without the proper papers.'

'As if we didn't know that,' shouted Grandpère, and others shouted with him.

Monsieur Sarthol held up his hands. 'There's more,' he said. 'There's more. I had him with me for half an hour inside the Mairie, and there's a lot more.' Hubert was picking the bark off his stick. 'He came to inform us that they are going to garrison Lescun. Within days there'll be a company of soldiers living here.' He went on over the hubbub. 'And from tonight onwards, he said, there's going to be round the clock patrols along the border – hundreds of soldiers posted all along the frontier. He made it quite plain to me that from now on no one would ever be able to escape into Spain. And he made it quite plain too that anyone helping fugitives will be shot.' The crowd was suddenly quiet. 'He means it. I'm telling you he means it. That poster there says he means it. Frenchmen, Jews, escaping prisoners-of-war, anyone – if you help them and you're caught you will be shot.' He stepped aside and pointed at the poster behind him. 'Just like those two. From Bedous they were. Patriç Léon and André Latour. I knew André, I knew him well, and so did most of you. They shot them last week. They were caught taking a family of Jews over the mountains into Spain.'

The crowd turned away, some crossing themselves, some murmuring prayers. Jo walked over to the poster and looked into the faces of the two men. They stared back at him, living eyes that were now dead. Hubert was beside him and he was crying. It was only at that moment that Jo realised that the war had come at last to Lescun, to his valley. Now and for the first time he understood the terrible danger that faced Widow Horcada and Benjamin if they were ever caught. Suddenly it was all real. This was the enemy his father had fought against. This was what happened when you lost a war and the enemy occupied your country.

He thought at once of going straight back up to Widow Horcada's house to warn them about the patrols on the border, to tell them about what had happened to the two men from Bedous, but he decided there was no immediate danger. After all the Germans had left the village, and besides he remembered the Widow saying that the children always rested up for a few days before Benjamin took them over the mountains. There was no hurry. Jo walked away from the poster and when he looked back into the Square Hubert was still standing there beside Monsieur Sarthol and Father Lasalle who were talking together. Suddenly Hubert lifted his stick, put it to his shoulder and pointed it down the road in the direction the armoured truck had taken. 'Bang!' he shouted. 'Bang! Bang! Bang! Bang!' Monsieur Sarthol swung round, pulled the stick out of his hand and broke it over his knee. Hubert hung his head and walked away.

'That Hubert,' said Maman that evening, 'he could have got himself killed.'

They were salting the cheeses, a job that Jo hated. The salt always found out a nick or a scratch in his hand and stung him.

'Maybe,' said Grandpère. 'Maybe. But he was just doing what all of us wanted to do if only we'd had the courage to do it.'

'And what good would that do?' said Maman. 'Tell me that. You shoot one of them and they shoot twenty of us. Haven't you heard what they've done?'

'There's always a price to be paid,' said Grandpère, wiping his hands with a cloth, 'and anyway you can't believe everything you hear. Those poor boys,' he went on, 'those poor, brave boys.'

'Brave and dead,' said Maman.

'Well, maybe it's better that way,' he said.

Jo had been thinking of other things. 'What's a Jew?' he asked.

'What?' said Maman.

'A Jew. Those two men who were shot. They were taking some Jews into Spain. That's what Monsieur Sarthol said.'

Grandpère and Maman looked at each other. For several moments neither seemed to know what to say.

'Well,' said Grandpère at last. 'It's difficult to say exactly what he is, your Jew. He's not a Christian that's for sure, and he's not a Catholic. He's not like you and me. Doesn't go to church.'

'They haven't got churches,' said Maman, 'they've got temples haven't they? In the Bible they've got temples. Solomon was a Jew, and David – all those people.'

'But why do the Germans want them?' said Jo. 'What did they do?'

Grandpère thought for a moment. 'Well,' he said.

'Hard to say. Hard to say. The Germans, they don't need much excuse do they? What they don't like they kill, and what they want they take. They don't need reasons, and even if they do they invent them as they go along.'

Christine shouted from upstairs, loudly and urgently. 'Oh that child. She'll drive me mad,' said Maman, blowing her hair back out of her eyes as she lifted another cheese on to the shelf. 'She's on the go from the minute she wakes up. Can I ride Rouf? Can I ride the donkey? Play with me, Maman. Play with me, Maman.' She sighed deeply. 'Jo, be a dear and see to her for me will you? We'll finish off here.' And she went on as Jo went out: 'Those soldiers today, they were so young.'

'They're old enough,' said Grandpère. 'Quite old enough.'

Jo lay awake for most of that night. Neither the wind that rattled the shutters, nor Christine's crying, nor his racing thoughts would let him sleep; and when he did drop off into a doze he was soon trying to extricate himself from a hideous, recurring dream. A rearing bear was chasing him remorselessly through the forest, through trees that seemed to clutch at him and tear at his clothes, trees that turned into black helmetted soldiers who caught him by the arms and held him fast and then stood him against a wall to be shot. Each time he managed to drag himself out of the dream just before they shot him and each time he determined to stay awake till dawn; but dawn was a long time coming that night. As he lay in the dark he began to worry that he should have warned Widow Horcada and Benjamin at once about the patrols on the border. He'd have to tell them just as soon as he could.

It was difficult to find time to get away without being missed. He was kept busy with sheep all morning, but at midday Grandpère left him alone with them on the hillside. 'Don't you go dropping off,' Grandpère said and he was gone. Sometimes Jo thought that Grandpère had guessed what had happened that day when the bear came. That wasn't the first time he'd hinted at it. He sat for some time on the rock and scanned the hills around him. His eyes came to rest on Widow Horcada's farm high above him. A vulture circled over the house and he watched it floating away over the trees beyond. He saw a shawl-wrapped figure come out of the door and cross the yard and he wondered which of them it was. He had to find a way to tell them but he could not leave the sheep. Had Hubert not come whistling by in mid-afternoon he would never have been able to leave them. Hubert was everyone's spare shepherd, particularly theirs, and he was good at it too. 'I'll only be half an hour or so,' said Jo, as Hubert settled down on the rock fixing his eyes on the sheep. He always took his job very seriously. Jo knew he would not move until he got back. He left him there grunting meaningfully at Rouf, who looked up at him with perfect understanding in his eyes.

Jo kept to the trees for as long as he could and then dashed out across the field towards the house. Widow Horcada was waiting for him in the yard leaning on her stick. She seemed surprised, even annoyed to see him.

'You,' she said. 'I thought I told you to stay away.'

'I had to come,' said Jo. 'I had to tell you.'

'Tell me what?' said Widow Horcada.

'The Germans, they were in the village yesterday. There's hundreds of them all along the frontier. I had to warn you.' Widow Horcada's eyes were suddenly wide with anxiety. 'And they've shot people too,' said Jo. 'Two of them from Bedous. They were helping Jews to escape over the mountains like Benjamin does.' He looked around. 'Where is Benjamin?'

'Gone,' said Widow Horcada. 'He saw the soldiers down another road. He went last night with Léah. He wouldn't wait. He thought they'd come searching the houses. I told him not to go, but he wouldn't listen. He wouldn't wait.' She looked up towards the mountains. 'Something's wrong, I know it is. He should be back by now. He should be back.'

CHAPTER 4

SOMEONE HAD TO GO AND FIND OUT WHAT HAD happened to them and Jo knew it would have to be him. There was no one else who could go. It was too far and too steep for Widow Horcada.

'Which way does he go?' Jo asked. 'The Col de Loraille?'

'Usually,' she said.

There were only a few hours of light left, he'd have to hurry. As he turned to go Widow Horcada caught him by the arm.

'You take care now, boy, d'you hear me?'

'Course,' he said and he was out of the door and running.

From the field below the house he could see Hubert

squatting on the rock, a hand on Rouf's neck. The sheep were spread out around him, yellow in the afternoon sun. Come the evening Hubert would drive the sheep home with Rouf. Jo had often gone off eagle watching and left Hubert to bring them in – he'd know what to do. Jo reached the trees and made his way through them down towards the river. From there on he'd be climbing all the way. He knew the path to the Col de Loraille well. It was the route up to their high summer pastures, to Papa's hut. The trees were loud with wind and the leaves were falling all about him. He followed the tumbling river upwards. Ahead of him, when the trees allowed, he could see the circle of sharp peaks at the head of the valley and above him the clouds raced each other back towards Lescun. He thought of shouting for them but he knew it would be pointless. Nothing could be heard over the roar of the river and the gusting wind. Every now and then he'd stop to scan the hills and woods about him. He saw a deer, but that was all. On and up he climbed until at last there were no trees above him, only the peaks and the sky. Dusk was beginning to settle. A flock of crows harried a lone buzzard towards the mountains. He looked about him for any sign of movement. There was nothing, only the buzzard and he seemed to be making for Spain, chased all the way by the marauding crows.

He disappeared over the peaks and the crows seemed satisfied with that for suddenly they broke off the chase and dispersed.

The sound of the shot came a moment later, echoing around the mountains. Without that Jo would never have seen the patrol. He crouched down behind a rock. There were three of them, three tiny dark figures moving slowly along the ridge against the skyline. A few of the crows settled on the ground now by Papa's hut and it occurred to him then that if Benjamin and Léah hadn't already been caught then they might be hiding up somewhere, and in that case there would be no better place than Papa's hut. The hut was several hundred metres away from him, built against a huge rock that had tumbled down the mountainside hundreds of years before. There were boulders strewn between him and the hut, boulders that he could use as cover; but even so he'd have to wait until the patrol had gone or until dark, whichever came first. For an hour or more the patrol moved slowly along the crest towards the Pic d'Anie and then the darkness thickened around him and he could see them no more.

The sliver of moon was for decoration only, it provided no light. It was safe enough to move now. Jo scuttled from boulder to boulder until he reached the hut. He whispered at the door as loud as he dared. 'Are you in there? Anyone in there?' But the reply came from behind him, from the donkey shed on the other side of the stream. It wasn't really a shed, just a cave in a rock with a half door across.

'Over here, Jo. We're over here.' It was Benjamin's voice.

He leapt the stream and picked his way over the rough ground towards the donkey shed.

'Inside!' said Benjamin opening the door and pulling Jo in. And then he saw Léah. She was backing away from him into the darkest corner of the shed. Benjamin limped after her leaning heavily on a stick.

'Don't mind her,' he said. 'She's frightened of her own shadow this one, but then she's got good cause.' It was some time before she could be persuaded to come out of her corner, and even then she wouldn't look at Jo but buried her head in Benjamin's coat. 'She's cold and she's tired, Jo,' he said, 'like me. We tried to cross last night. And we'd have made it too.'

'What happened?' said Jo.

'My ankle, my confounded ankle, that's what happened.' He stroked Léah's hair and hugged her close to him. 'We had the perfect night for it. Lots of clouds, plenty of wind; but soldiers, soldiers every-where. I must have been over these mountains a dozen times now and I've never seen so many soldiers. That's why we were running. We don't normally run. It's always quieter if you walk. I don't know if it was a stone or a hole in the ground, it doesn't matter anyway. Somehow or other I turned my ankle over, you could hear it go – like a gunshot it was – and now it's blown up like a balloon. Anyway, we couldn't go on any further so all day we've been cooped up in here waiting for the soldiers to go. We were going to try to make it back on our own after dark, but I don't think we'd ever have done it, not on our own.'

'Is it broken?' Jo asked.

'Perhaps, but anyway it won't be much use to me for a few months, that's for sure.' He bent over and kissed Léah on the top of her head. She looked up at him. 'It'll get better – God willing – and when it does we'll try again. I don't care how many soldiers they put on those mountains, we'll find a way past them. Now Jo,' he said, reaching out and putting a hand on his shoulder, 'I'm going to need someone strong to lean on.' He turned to Léah and spoke in another language. Léah looked from Benjamin to Jo and back again. Benjamin nodded and nudged her forward. She reached out slowly and Jo took her hand. 'All clear outside is it?' said Benjamin. Jo peered out. He could hear nothing and see nothing. He felt Léah's cold fingers gripping tighter.

'All clear,' he said, and with Benjamin's arm hooked around his neck they walked out into the night.

It was a slow and painful journey down the mountain. Benjamin may have been a small man but he was heavy enough and Jo's shoulder ached under his weight. He had to tread very carefully for he knew that if he stumbled they would all fall like a pack of cards. Léah clung to Jo's free hand and even on the narrowest tracks nothing could persuade her to let go and follow along behind. Any sudden jolt and Jo could hear the stifled groan, and feel the grip tighten around his shoulder. They stopped to rest by the river knowing that the worst part – the uphill part – still lay ahead. From now on Benjamin needed Léah too as a crutch, but even with one hand on her shoulder and an arm around Jo he had to put some weight on his useless foot. Every step was an agony to him, an agony Jo suffered with him.

Jo took them the quickest way up the hillside, across the open fields. There was no thought in his mind now of avoiding German patrols or of meeting anyone else for that matter; and clearly Benjamin felt the same for he began to sing, softly at first, through clenched teeth, and then within moments Léah's thin piping voice joined his. It was a slow, martial song, with a simple rhythmic tune that Jo soon picked up as well. That song with its regular, defiant beat kept them going all the way up to the house and by then they were singing out loud against the wind. A shadow came out from behind the barn and became Widow Horcada.

She took Benjamin's outstretched hand. 'We're all right, Grandmère,' he said, 'we're all right.' And Jo found himself suddenly and blissfully free of Benjamin's weight as Widow Horcada put her arms around him to support him.

'I'd better be getting back,' said Jo, rubbing his shoulder. 'They'll be wondering.'

'Bless you, Jo,' said Widow Horcada. It was the first time she'd ever called him 'Jo'.

'I told you, didn't I?' said Benjamin. 'I said this boy was a good one.' He bent down and whispered something to Léah.

'*Dziękuję*, Jo' she said, and her face broke at last into a shy smile.

'What does that mean?' Jo asked.

'It means "thank you" in Polish,' said Benjamin.

They were waiting up for him when he got home. Jo had made up his story on the way back. It wasn't difficult. It was a story he'd used often when he'd been late in, but then the story had often been true, or part of it anyway, and he'd never been this late. He'd seen the eagle again, he said, whilst he was out guarding the sheep and then Hubert had come along so he'd left him with the sheep. He'd followed the eagle all the way down the valley and up into the mountains to see if he could find its nesting site, then he'd lost his way in the dark on the way back. 'It's very dark out there,' he said.

Grandpère was frowning at him. 'Eagles don't nest in the Autumn, do they?' he said.

'Course not,' Jo went on, 'but I thought if I could find where it settled, then next Spring I'd know where to look. I've been looking for their nest for ages, you know I have.'

'Never mind about the eagle,' said Maman. 'What about the patrols? Didn't you hear what Monsieur Sarthol said. Didn't you? I've been worried sick, Jo.'

'I never saw anything,' said Jo.

'Your mother's told you. She's told you time and again, you're not to go off like that without telling her.' Grandpère was playing stern – he wasn't very good at it. 'You wouldn't have dared do it if your father was here, would you?' And Jo couldn't argue with that. He kept quiet, it was the best way. In the end they both ran out of admonishments as he knew they would, but more important they had not doubted his story and his secret was safe.

'Papa's written again,' said Maman pulling a card out of her pocket. They'd had cards like this before. It was a filled-in form, not a letter at all. Jo recognised Papa's handwriting. It said what all the others had said, that he was well, that he was still working in a timber yard and that was about all. 'Three years he's been gone now,' said Maman, 'nearly three years.'

'He'll be back Lise,' said Grandpère.

'Will he?' she said, shaking her head. 'Not if this war goes on like it is. They'll never let him come home, never.' Jo hated to see the tears in Maman's eyes and looked away. 'You know the worst thing,' she said, 'it's that I don't know where he is. If I knew where he was, if I could look at a map and say "he's there, that's where he is", that'd be something.'

'Off to bed, Jo,' said Grandpère, 'you've got school tomorrow. And no more chasing after your eagles, d'you hear me?' And he slapped Jo playfully on the bottom as he went out.

It was always the same whenever a card came from Papa. In between whiles they hardly ever talked about him. It wasn't that he was forgotten exactly. He just wasn't there, that's all. They'd all had to get along without him and they'd managed to do it partly because they didn't think about him; but whe ever his cards came Maman would become morose and silent for days afterwards and that would upset everyone in the house, everyone except Grandpère – only the Germans seemed capable of upsetting Grandpère.

The next morning Hubert was waiting for him outside as he was most mornings. He liked to walk to school with Jo because he always had done. He was too old for school now but Monsieur Audap would let him sit at the back and make his miniatures. He even provided him with the bread. Hubert was never any trouble except for the occasional sound of spitting, and everyone ignored even that by now. Hubert's miniatures were made out of bread. He would cut open a loaf, pull out the soft bread and discard the crust. Then he would knead it into a thick paste, spitting on it all the time. He would roll it out until it was wafer thin and cut out the shapes he wanted. Somehow this unpromising material would be transformed into minute cups and bowls and chalices. When Hubert had finished modelling them, he would press them with the point of a hot iron until they were hard. It was a marvel that his great hands, that seemed often so clumsy, could produce such delicate work. Afterwards, when they had dried out, he would paint them with a fine brush, varnish them and then give them to his friends or to his father, whose house was full of them. Jo had twenty-one of them on the shelf in his bedroom, each one different from the other. They were a testament to a long and lasting friendship, and Jo treasured them.

Monsieur Audap liked to have Hubert in the school, everyone did. There wasn't an ounce of malice in him. The little children liked him because he would let them climb on him at playtime. The great game was to try and sit on Hubert to keep him down, and he'd struggle and struggle and rise up like a giant and discard them in all directions. Then they'd climb on again and try to haul him down, and in the end he'd let them, and they'd have their triumph. The older children were half afraid of him – Jo too if he was honest. Some, like Laurent, would mock him occasionally, but only from behind his back. And even then they respected him and not just for his size but because Hubert was always game – he would always join in whatever was going on. He was like a chameleon; whatever they were – pirates, soldiers, Red Indians – he would be too. When they were happy, he was happy; and if someone was sad then he'd sit beside them and share in their wretchedness. And without exception everyone admired his handiwork. Monsieur Audap said that one day people would go to see it in an exhibition in Paris, it was that good and no one doubted it.

Hubert was sitting at the back of the class intent on his latest minute bowl, his eyes close to his fingers, when Armand Jollet burst into the classroom. He took Monsieur Audap by the elbow and led him towards the door. Both were talking in excited whispers. Monsieur Audap saw him out and then he called for Hubert, who was reluctant at first to leave his bowl.

'Now, Hubert!' said Monsieur Audap clapping his hands, and Hubert left his desk at once, wiping his hands on his trousers. 'The drum, Hubert,' he said and Hubert's eyes lit up; he loved his drum. For the children any interruption to lessons was always welcome, but when Hubert was being sent out around with the drum that meant something exciting had happened, something important even. By the time they were all gathered outside they could hear Hubert's drumming echoing around the village. Monsieur Audap lined them up in twos. They always went with the same partners. Jo went with Laurent, they had done since they were little, and they walked in a long crocodile down towards the Square. People were running out of their houses, pulling on their coats as they came. No one knew what was going on, not until they reached the Square.

Soldiers were drawn up in front of the Mairie, two ranks of them in grey uniforms. They wore side caps not helmets. In front of them, on a bay horse, was an officer, both hands on his reins, a revolver in his belt. Hubert's drumming came ever closer as more people came crowding into the Square. Monsieur Sarthol, the tricolour of office around his waist, was standing beside the officer reading some papers. Jo found his view blocked so he climbed up on to the railings behind the war memorial just as Hubert, still drumming enthusiastically, came marching down into the Square. Grandpère, with Rouf beside him, was leaning against a wall studying the soldiers critically. The Mayor told Hubert to stop, but Hubert was so intent upon his drumming that he did not hear his father's command. Armand Jollet tapped him on the shoulder and shook his head. Hubert stopped drumming. The officer waited until everyone was quiet before he began to speak. His accent was heavy but he spoke slowly and Jo could understand every word.

'My name is Lieutenant Weissmann,' he said. He spoke in a reedy voice, a voice that seemed to complement him perfectly. He was lean and long and lanky. 'I have been sent here to Lescun to guard this sector of the Frontier. My men and I will be billetted in the priest's house by the church. We will be living amongst you for some time and we wish to do so as peaceably as possible. I can assure you that we will not intrude into your lives unless you compel us to.' The horse tossed his head as the officer spoke, his bit jangling. He began to paw at the ground. The soldiers were not like the ones who'd come before. These were older men, some portly even, and with grey hair. Their boots were dusty and they looked somehow awkward in their uniforms. These were men dressed up as soldiers, not the real thing. The Lieutenant went on.

'There are certain rules, however, that must be obeyed. First, there will be a strict curfew. This means that after half past nine at night no one is allowed out of their houses. Of course passes must be carried by everyone at all times. And lastly, all firearms, hunting rifles, shotguns and so on, must be handed in by six o'clock this evening – for safekeeping you understand. I repeat, we are here to guard the Frontier. Too many people have been escaping across into Spain. You all know what will happen if you are caught helping those wishing to escape. I have to tell you we want no unpleasantness but we have our job to do and we will do it. Thank you for your attention.' He pointed to the ground by the horse's feet. 'Six o'clock. You will leave your rifles here. My men will be here to receive them. That is all.' He turned to face the soldiers. There were barked commands and they marched across the Square and up the road towards the church, their rifles slung on their shoulders.

'I won't do it, Jo,' said Grandpère as they drove the sheep down from the fields later that afternoon. 'I won't do it I tell you. They march in here like they own the place. They kick Father Lasalle out of his house and tell us we mustn't go out after dark. What are we, children? Be good boys, hand in your guns. Who the hell do they think they are? Ah, they're polite enough these Germans. They say their pleases and afterwards they'll say their thankyous. All very polite I'm sure, but they can afford to be can't they?' It was a monologue that lasted all the way home.

Hubert was waiting for them kicking his heels on the wall. He jumped down to let the sheep in through the gate. At that moment three soldiers came round the corner, marching in step, their packs on their backs. They waited and watched as Hubert and Rouf drove the sheep into the yard. Jo saw that the tallest of them had stripes on his shoulders. He was head and shoulders above the others and wore his side cap at a jaunty angle. He had a drooping black moustache that was too small for his face. Jo caught his eye and the soldier smiled and waved at him cheerily; and then they were gone. Grandpère gripped his arm.

'Don't you go smiling at them,' he said. 'The last

thing we want to do is make them feel at home.'

'I wasn't,' said Jo, and that was the truth. And yet he had wanted to return the smile. 'I was just looking,' he said.

The grip on Jo's arm tightened and Grandpère began to chuckle. 'They want rifles, don't they?' he said. 'Well, I'll give them a rifle. Wait here.' And he opened the gate and walked through the sheep into the barn. Moments later he came back out again and Jo understood at once what he was going to do. He was carrying the ancient muzzle-loading rifle they kept above the fireplace in the kitchen, the one his great-grandfather had used in an old war a long time ago – or so the story went. He handed it to Hubert, who beamed and put it to his shoulder and aimed at a high flying crow. 'Bang,' he said. 'Bang, bang.'

'You can't give them that,' said Jo.

'And why not? It's what they asked for. They wanted rifles didn't they?' He turned to Hubert. 'It's not for you, Hubert; it's for them, for the Boche.' And the smile left Hubert's face. 'Here, feel this Jo,' Grandpère went on, and he took Jo's hand and pressed it against his side. Jo could feel the barrel of his hunting rifle through the coat. 'Just in case they ever come searching – and they will, you can be sure of that – I'm going to hide this somewhere they'll never find it, somewhere they'll never even think of looking. Come on. You come too Hubert, I need you.' Hubert looked delighted again. He always loved to feel wanted, to feel useful.

They made their way up around the back of the village and came down behind the churchyard. Grandpère sat on the wall and looked about him, then he swung his legs over and let himself down the other side. The family tomb was on the far side of the graveyard overlooking the valley – the best view in the graveyard Grandpère always said. They crouched down behind the tomb and Grandpère opened his coat. He took the rifle out and leaned it carefully against a grey marble slab that served as the lid of the tomb.

'Here, give us a hand,' he said. The slab moved much more easily than Jo expected. 'That's far enough,' Grandpère said, looking around him. He plunged his hand into his coat pocket and came out with a single bullet. He held it up between his thumb and his forefinger. His voice was steely, as Jo had never heard it before. 'When the time comes, if the time comes, then at least I'll be taking one of them with me,' and he slipped the bullet in and rammed the bolt home. He wrapped it carefully in a cloth and let it down into the tomb, peering in after it. 'That'll do,' he said, and they heaved and shoved until the marble slab was back in place. 'Now,' said Grandpère wiping his hands together and grinning mischievously, 'now they can have their rifle. We'll give it to them personally.' And he picked up the ancient, rusted rifle, and they followed him through the back door of the church, down the dark aisle and out of the front door into the sunlight beyond.

There were two soldiers standing in the Square, half a dozen or so rifles lying on the ground at their feet. Grandpère walked right up to them. For several silent moments he looked them up and down, almost as if he was inspecting them, first one and then the other.

'Good evening,' he said at last. 'You wanted this, I believe,' and he laid the rifle down on top of the others.

The soldiers looked down at it and then at Grandpère; they seemed uncertain of what to do. 'It needs oiling from time to time,' said Grandpère. 'Make sure you look after it.' One of the soldiers was about to say something but Grandpère turned and walked away. When Jo looked back both the soldiers were gazing after them.

'I enjoyed that,' said Grandpère as they rounded the corner, and the smile on his face set Hubert laughing, and when Hubert laughed he laughed with his whole being and you had to laugh with him.

They were passing the baker's shop, Grandpère still chuckling, when Jo saw Widow Horcada. She was coming slowly towards them, her head down so you could only see the top of her shawl. She had a basket over each arm.

Grandpère held out his arms. 'Alice,' he shouted. 'You're looking younger than ever.'

She smiled as he came towards her. He kissed her warmly on both cheeks. 'Go on with you, you old goat,' she said, pushing him away, and then she looked at him quizzically. 'What're you looking so pleased about anyway?'

'That's our little secret, isn't it boys?' said Grandpère, taking Widow Horcada's arm. 'We're all allowed our little secrets, eh?'

She tried to shake him off. 'Henri! What will people think?'

'Let them think what they like,' said Grandpère. 'I'm too old to care and so are you.' Madame Soulet was at the door of her baker's shop, her mouth open. Grandpère bowed at her with a flourish. 'I shall carry your shopping, Madame. I shall escort you home.'

At that moment they heard the sound of laughter and a couple of soldiers came out of the Square towards them. They stopped at the corner to light each other's cigarettes.

'I heard they were here,' said Widow Horcada. 'How many of them are there?'

'There's twenty-two of the beggars,' said Grand-père, 'and a horse. They mean business. I tell you one thing, no one's ever going to get over those mountains again, not now.'

'That's your grandson isn't it?' said Widow Horcada. Jo dared not look her in the eye. 'Doesn't have much to say for himself does he?' Grandpère nudged him.

'Good morning, Madame,' said Jo.

'Strong boy is he?'

'Course he is,' said Grandpère and he squeezed Jo's shoulder approvingly. 'From good stock he is.'

The Widow Horcada nodded. 'You wouldn't like to lend him to me?' she said, wrinkling her nose and sniffing.

'Lend him?'

'Once a week say. He could bring me my shopping. It's climbing these hills, Henri – down's worse than up. My old knees aren't what they were.'

'I don't know,' said Grandpère. 'It's a bit difficult just at the moment, what with his father being away. Don't know if we can spare him.'

'I'll tell you what I'll do,' said Widow Horcada. 'I'll pay him, a kilo of honey every week. How's that? It won't take but an hour or two. Help me out it would.'

'Once a week you say?' said Grandpère. 'Well, I expect we could manage that. What do you think, Jo?'

Jo nodded. 'When would you want him to start?'

'Now,' said Widow Horcada, and she held out the largest basket. 'Well, come along boy, I won't eat you. Come along.'

Grandpère laughed as they walked away. 'Mind you pay him now,' he called after them; and Jo followed the Widow in silence out of the village.

They were off the track and into the fields before she said a word. She put down her basket and bent over, her hands on her knees, breathing hard.

'Are you all right?' Jo asked.

She nodded and looked up. 'I'm sorry, Jo,' she said. 'But you're the only one that knows, you're the only one I could ask. It's not that I don't trust your grandfather but the fewer that know the less dangerous it is.' She straightened up slowly. 'We've got five of them now, Jo. Five children to look after, and there's more on the way. Benjamin's still laid up with his ankle; he can't even stand up, but even if he was fit they'd never make it over the mountains, not now, not with all these soldiers about. What can we do? We can't send the children back where they've come from, and we can't take them where they want to go.' She fanned her face with the corner of her shawl. 'I don't know what I'm going to do, Jo. I don't know how long I can keep them all fed. And that Armand Jollet at the shop, he's becoming suspicious, I know he is. You can't blame him – I've never bought so much in all my life; and what I do buy I can't carry, not on my own, Jo. I'm just not strong enough any more. I'm going to need all the help you can give me.'

CHAPTER 5

HOSTILITY TOWARDS THE GERMAN OCCUPIERS was silent, but as time passed they were proving more and more difficult to hate. They were tactful, unobtrusive even. No houses had been searched. No foreign flags of occupation fluttered over the village. Lieutenant Weissmann seemed as good as his word. The two communities existed side by side separately, ignoring each other respectfully. Some of the soldiers came to church on Sundays, Lieutenant Weissman amongst them. Father Lasalle loved to play the organ and it seemed that Lieutenant Weissmann shared his passion. Father Lasalle was only too pleased to let him practise on the church organ. Many of the soldiers came to the café in the evening but even there they sat apart, at first anyway. It soon became apparent though that two or three of them had fought at the Battle of Verdun in the First World War and it was not long before ancient enemies were exchanging reminiscences across the café, and with no rancour on either side. On the contrary their shared suffering seemed to banish mutual reserve and suspicion.

Jo wouldn't have believed it possible had he not witnessed it himself but even Grandpère was drawn into a moment of nostalgic self-indulgence. Jo was coming out of school one lunchtime when he caught sight of Grandpère outside the café. He was deep in conversation with a German soldier. He towered over Grandpère, a great tree of a man. He had stripes on his uniform, a Corporal, Grandpère had said. Besides Lieutenant Weissmann, the Corporal was the only soldier who spoke good French and he lost no opportunity to practise it on the children with whom he had already become a firm favourite, mostly because he seemed to have an endless supply of sweets. He had offered one to Jo only a few days before. Jo had taken it but then his conscience had got the better of him and he spat it out around the corner, something he immediately regretted as he watched Rouf enjoying it instead.

The Corporal smiled at Jo as he saw him coming

and Grandpère looked somewhat shamefaced. On the way home he explained.

'It's hard to believe,' he said, 'but that Corporal and me, we were very likely shooting at each other at Verdun.' He shook his head. 'Just sixteen he was then. Invalided out same as me.' And then he caught Jo's eye and was silent.

This reunion of old soldiers broke the last of the ice and thereafter the village settled and adapted to the new normality of being occupied.

Hubert had seemed more resentful than most at first, and because he had no inhibitions was by far the most daring. He was always blowing raspberries at them in the street but the Germans simply laughed and blew raspberries back at him. It became a tit-for-tat game that Hubert enjoyed and they enjoyed. Before long they all knew his name. They would give him chocolate and they let him groom Lieutenant Weissmann's horse. Hubert was happy, and whoever made Hubert happy struck a common chord with the spirit of the village.

Jo had never much liked Armand Jollet before he shot the bear and he liked him even less now. With the arrival of the Germans his shop was doing well, very well. The soldiers had money to spend and nowhere else to spend it but the café and the shop. The Jollet family owned them both. No one else in the village stooped to fawning except Armand Jollet. He would always accompany the soldiers to the door of his shop and open it for them. He would bow and scrape in a manner that made Jo cringe to watch him; and these days Jo was often in the shop to pick up Widow Horcada's provisions. Twice a week it was now, in all weathers, he climbed the hillside, his arms aching under the weight of the baskets. There were eight children up there now Widow Horcada told him. Jo had never set eyes on any of them except Léah and he hadn't seen her for some time. He longed to sneak into the barn and take a look but he knew he shouldn't. It was Benjamin who usually came to the door to take the baskets from him. He was still hobbling on his bad ankle. Jo was always invited in but he was never allowed to stay for long in the warmth of the kitchen. 'Your honey, Jo,' the Widow would say, pushing it across the table towards him. 'And here's the list for next time.' And then he'd find himself out in the yard again facing a closed door. He knew why he could not stay. Being inclined to repeat herself she had told him several times. 'You've got to remember, Jo,' she'd said, 'to everyone in the village you're just an unwilling delivery boy for the Black Widow. God knows who's watching your comings and your goings, but that's just what you must do, come and go. We don't want people asking questions do we? It's best that way.' Jo knew she was right but it hurt him just the same; and questions were beginning to be asked anyway, questions he could not answer.

One afternoon that winter, Monsieur Jollet caught him by the arm as he was leaving the shop: 'You know what she's doing with all this food?' Jo looked away. 'She's up to something isn't she?'

At that moment the door opened and the Corporal came in, his moustache white with snow. 'Jo, isn't it?' he said, stamping the snow off his boots. 'Whenever I see you, you are carrying those baskets. You have a big family?' Jo said nothing.

'It's for Madame Horcada, Corporal,' said Armand Jollet. 'Jo does her fetching and carrying for her. She lives on her own but there's food enough there for a family of ten. I think she's storing it up for the winter, like a squirrel.' And he laughed a high-pitched, nervous laugh. 'And how can I help you, Corporal?'

'Cigarettes,' said the Corporal and then he turned to Jo. 'One minute, Jo, I'll give you a hand. It's slippery out there.' The Corporal paid for his cigarettes, Armand Jollet counting out his change rather too meticulously and finishing with a flurry of thankyous before showing them out.

The snow floated down in huge flakes. The Corporal insisted on carrying both the baskets. He had his head back and his tongue out to catch the snowflakes. He caught several before he got one in the eye and broke into laughter. 'It makes me feel as if I am at home,' he said. Jo walked along beside him searching his mind for some way of extricating himself from the situation.

'This Widow,' said the Corporal, 'where does she live?'

'Up in the hills outside the village,' Jo said and he reached for the baskets. 'I can manage, honestly I can.' But the Corporal would not let him take them.

'How far?'

'Three, maybe four kilometres.'

'That's not so far,' said the Corporal and they walked on. 'Bavaria, you know it?' Jo shook his head. 'In Germany, in the south of Germany. It's where I live, in a village like this, like Lescun. There are mountains all about just like these. I'm a forester, Jo, so for me you understand this is like home.'

Jo was desperately trying to think of a way to get rid of him. 'If she sees you,' said Jo, 'I won't get my honey.' It was weak but it was all he could think of.

'Honey?'

'She pays me. Widow Horcada, she pays me in

honey, and if she sees you carrying the baskets for me she won't pay me.'

'I haven't had honey since I left home,' said the Corporal. 'Acacia honey and apple blossom honey, that's what we have at my home. My wife, she makes it. Of course the bees make it but she looks after the bees. And my children, they love it. They eat it so fast I am lucky if they leave me the spoon to lick. They're all girls, my children. Three of them. Can you imagine that, Jo? Four girls in one house and me? No honey and no peace.' His face was suddenly serious. 'I never thought I'd miss them so much. One of them, she has gone to Berlin to work the telephones. She's the clever one.' He stopped and put down the baskets. 'These baskets, they are heavy. There is enough in here to feed the five thousand.'

Jo saw his opportunity and picked them up at once. 'Thanks,' he said. 'I can take them now.'

'Very well,' said the Corporal, 'but one day, one day I must taste your honey, yes?' He looked up through the falling snow at the mountains around them. 'I am like a bear,' said the Corporal laughing. 'I like honey, and I like mountains. I like snow. We have bears in my mountains too you know; and eagles, we have eagles.'

'So have we,' said Jo.

'I know,' said the Corporal. 'I have seen them,

and vultures too. Have you ever seen eagles through binoculars, Jo?'

'No.'

'In the spring, Jo, we go up the mountains together, you and me; and we look at eagles with my binoculars, yes? With binoculars you can see an eagle close as your nose, just like you can reach out and touch it. It's a promise, yes?' And the Corporal turned and walked away.

Once inside the warmth of the farmhouse Jo did not want to leave, and for a change they did not seem to want him to either. They sat him down over a bowl of hot soup which he blew on to steam his face warm. He had almost finished wiping his bread around the bowl when he realised that no-one was saying anything. With his mouth still full of bread he looked from one to the other and waited. It was clear they had something to tell him.

'Jo,' said Benjamin, 'I know you have done a lot for us already,' and as he spoke he walked slowly over to the stove, leaning for support on the backs of the chairs as he went. He turned round and faced him, his face serious, 'and we don't like to ask you.'

'Ask me what?'

'We need money, Jo,' said Widow Horcada. 'We just haven't got the money to go on buying food. There's ten of them in the barn now. They've eaten me out of house and home. The cow's gone dry so there's no milk any more. I haven't even got any honey left to pay you. I've got enough money to last another week and that'll be the end of it.' She sank back in her chair. 'There's only one thing we can do, Jo. I've got to sell my pigs. The children won't eat them and Benjamin won't eat them – it's against their religion – and I can't afford to go on feeding them. With the money they make we can go on for a few more months maybe. So they'll have to go. But I'm not selling them to anyone, Jo. Those pigs, they're like family to me. There's only one other person knows enough about pigs in this valley and that's Henri, your grandfather. Always used to keep pigs when he was a young man and he was good at it too. The trouble is he's not going to buy them without seeing them is he? And that's what I want you to do, Jo. I want you to bring him up here.' Jo looked across at Benjamin. 'Don't you worry nothing about him,' Widow Horcada went on, 'he'll be well out of sight, same as the children. Henri won't know anything, and what he won't know can't hurt him, can it? So, the next time you come up here with the shopping – that'll be next Wednesday afternoon won't it? – I want you to bring your grandfather with you.'

'What am I going to tell him?' asked Jo.

'Tell him I'm too old, tell him I can't get about like I used to – that'll be true enough. Tell him what you like, Jo, but get him here.'

'Can you do it, Jo?' Benjamin said.

'I'll try,' said Jo.

And he tried that evening whilst Maman was upstairs putting Christine to bed.

'What? All of them?' said Grandpère, and he was frowning as he lit his cigarette and coughed the match out.

'That's what she told me,' said Jo. 'She told me she's too old to go on.'

Grandpère shook his head. 'Doesn't make sense. Doesn't make sense any of it. She's always had pigs up there, and her father before her. She loves those pigs like her own children. She'd never sell them, not unless she had to, I know she wouldn't. I tell you, Jo, if she gives up her pigs that'll be the end of her. She'll have nothing left to live for.'

'Perhaps she needs the money,' said Jo.

'Well I'd like to know what for,' Grandpère said, 'after all, she's only got herself to look after hasn't she? She's been careful all her life. I just can't understand it. Still,' he said, smiling through the cigarette smoke, 'that's the first invitation I've had from her in nigh on fifty years so I'll go.' He leaned forward and spoke low.

'But don't you go telling your mother, Jo. She doesn't like her, and what's worse she doesn't like me to like her. There's stories about me and the old Widow – not true of course – but if I know your mother she'll start thinking her thoughts, so not a word, eh?' Jo was quite used by now to keeping secrets. One more would not be that difficult.

Rouf followed them that Wednesday afternoon but Jo did not notice him until it was too late. He tried to send him back but he wouldn't go. You could never make Rouf do anything he didn't want to do. They were walking across Widow Horcada's back yard when he saw Rouf sniffing along the barn wall towards the door. When he reached it he stopped, his nose thrust under the door and snuffling noisily. Then he began to scratch at it and whine.

'What's up with that dog?' said Grandpère and then the door of the house opened and Widow Horcada was there.

'I'll take those,' she said looking at Jo hard, and she almost snatched the baskets out of his hands. 'You can take that dog home, Jo.' She spoke sharply. 'You know I don't like dogs around my place.' She looked at Grandpère. 'Well, don't just stand there, Henri, come along in and shut the door behind you.'

It was all Jo could do to drag Rouf away from the

barn door. He had to drive him down the hillside from behind like a sheep. Jo would have given anything to stay behind and listen to what was going on. He wondered where Benjamin would be hiding – in the barn perhaps, with the children, he thought, to keep them calm. If so, then Rouf's snuffling must have shaken them all rigid. But wherever they all were they must have kept well hidden, and whatever money arrangements they came to inside the house must have been satisfactory for Grandpère was quite evidently delighted when he came back. He told Maman that evening that pigs would be in great demand now. The Boche eat a lot of pork. He could fatten them on the sheeps' whey for practically nothing. He would hardly have to buy any feed for them, he said. 'But they smell,' Maman protested. 'Pig smell, you can never wash it off.' But Grandpère managed to persuade her it was a smell they could learn to live with. Christine was delighted with the idea – she'd never ridden a pig.

The next day as Jo came tramping home from school through the village he saw Hubert and Grand-père coming down the road driving the pigs in front of them, or trying to. It was all going fine until they reached the Square and the pigs set off at a trot. They went running off in all directions, squealing and grunting as they explored every front door and every drainpipe. It took half the village and a few of the soldiers as well to round them all up and drive them back to Jo's house where they managed to pen them all in, all except one – a large determined sow with pink and swinging teats – that Jo had to chase all the way to the church and back before she at last gave up and reluctantly joined her friends.

Grandpère's new pigs had become the talk of the village. After church on Sunday there were dark whisperings that Henri Lalande had bought the Widow's pigs for reasons that were not entirely agricultural or commercial. There was much tutting and shaking of heads and some smirking mirth too. Jo overheard Madame Soulet in the street saying that Henri Lalande must be out of his mind. 'At his age!' she said. 'At his age!'

At school Laurent snorted at Jo now whenever he met him, and 'oink oink' became the new greeting amongst the children until the joke wore thin. Maman declared that the sheep were giving less milk now that the pigs were about the place, but Grandpère just smiled and said that they'd soon settle down; and sure enough they did.

With the end of the snows the sheep were being moved each day to and from the pastures around the village and the sound of their bells in the fields heralded the first edelweiss and the first larks. You didn't have to go out into the countryside though to know it was spring. When Father Lasalle left the church door open so that the sound of his organ playing could be heard all over the village, everyone knew for sure that Winter was behind them.

Monsieur Audap took advantage of the warming sun to lead the class out on the spring expedition. He did this once for every season of the year, and the children looked forward to it more even than a holiday. It was like a treasure hunt. They scoured the slopes looking for plants and insects, footprints and droppings. Everything they found was recorded and sketched. There wasn't a plant Monsieur Audap could not name, nor a footprint nor a dropping he could not identify.

The great find of the day was a bear print in the muddy beach down by the river. It was Laurent who found it first – Laurent found most things first. Everyone thought it was another of his practical jokes. 'A bear!' he cried. 'It's got to be.' And Monsieur Audap confirmed it. 'A front paw,' he said, 'and a small one at that; but it's a bear right enough, a young one I'd say. Look at the claw marks.'

'What's the matter, Jo?' said Laurent clapping him on the back. 'You look as if you've seen a ghost.' They hunted up and down the river bank for more prints but they found none. 'A one-footed bear,' said Laurent hopping beside Jo on the way back that afternoon, but Jo found it difficult to enjoy the joke. 'Cheer up Jo,' he said. Jo smiled as best he could but it was not very convincing and he knew it.

They sang songs all the way back to the village, Monsieur Audap waving his hand above his head conducting them. As they came round the last bend in the road they saw a German patrol coming towards them. 'Sing up, sing up,' said Monsieur Audap, and they swung past the patrol in full voice. Jo enjoyed the moment, they all did. It was a little victory but even a little victory was better than none at all.

They were still in high spirits when they came into the village. Perhaps that was why Laurent put his tongue out at Madame Soulet as she was arranging baguettes in the window of her shop. She came rushing out after Monsieur Audap complaining bitterly and pointing at Laurent. After they got back to school Laurent was called into Monsieur Audap's room and Jo noticed that when he came out he was only just smiling. Monsieur Audap had clearly said his piece – and he had a way of reaching his mark.

It was that interview that goaded Laurent into an act of revenge and for that he needed an accomplice.

'I need someone with a deep voice, Jo,' he said, 'and that means you.' It was never easy to say no to Laurent. Always good friends, with both their fathers prisoners-of-war in Germany, they had become even closer allies. Jo was left with no choice in the matter. 'We'll meet at my place,' said Laurent, 'just before curfew.'

'What for?' Jo asked.

'For a bit of fun,' Laurent said. 'I'll teach the old bat. I'll teach her.'

Jo knew well enough which 'old bat' he was talking about but until he got to Laurent's house that night he had no idea what she was going to be taught.

'I can see her from my window. I've watched her,' said Laurent. 'She always comes out of Madame Robbé's house between twenty past and half past nine. She walks across the Square and then back to her place, regular as clockwork. You know what you've got to do?' Jo didn't want to do it, not because he didn't dare – there was nothing very daring about it – he just didn't think they could pull it off; but Laurent ignored all his doubts and protests.

Laurent tested the torch and they crept out together into the dark streets. Once in place they crouched down behind a wall and waited. Jo had been rehearsed in his part but as the door of the Robbés' house opened and he heard Madame Soulet's shrill voice he found that his brain was suddenly frozen, that he could no longer remember his words. The door closed plunging the Square into darkness again. The moment had come. Laurent waited until the footsteps were just the other side of the wall and then he stood up, shining his torch directly into Madame Soulet's eyes. Laurent had to kick Jo into action. Jo cleared his throat.

'Halt,' he said in his deepest voice. 'Ihre Papiere bitte.' And then in his best gutteral German accent, 'Your papers please.' Jo looked up from his crouching position under the wall. Madame Soulet was holding up her hand trying to keep the light out of her eyes and she was stammering with terror. She held out her papers, her hand trembling. Laurent took them, glanced at them perfunctorily and handed them back quickly. 'Gut, sehr gut,' said Jo as rehearsed. 'Gute Nacht.' And she hurried away whimpering into the dark, Laurent's torch beam following her all the way to her door. When she had gone in Laurent bent over the wall and put his hands over his mouth to stop himself laughing out loud. Jo took the torch out of his hand and switched it off.

'Did you see her face?' said Laurent. 'Did you see it? You were brilliant, Jo, brilliant.' And then from the darkness behind them came a soft voice.

'*Ausgezeichnet.*' Jo's heart leapt into his mouth. 'A brilliant performance as you said.' They turned and the torch beam hit their faces full on. '*Ihre Papiere bitte,*' said the voice. It was Lieutenant Weissmann.

'I haven't got them on me,' said Laurent.

'*Und du?*' The torch came full beam on Jo's face. Jo shook his head. He could just make out a shadow behind the torch and the outline of a head against the sky. 'Turn around,' said Lieutenant Weissmann. They obeyed. '*Hände Hoch.* Hands up.' He kicked Laurent first and Jo waited for his turn. When it came it was more than a playful kick in the pants. It hurt just enough to carry a meaning. 'Do not do it again,' said Lieutenant Weissmann. 'You understand me? You have one and a half minutes before curfew. *Schnell*!' They climbed the wall and ran home going their different directions. Jo did not stop until he'd shut the door behind him and even then his heart could not stop pounding in his ears.

Whenever Jo went up to Widow Horcada's farm with the shopping now Benjamin would put on his shawl and come out into the yard to see him off. He would walk up and down to show him how much he was improving and each time he walked more easily. First the stick went and then within weeks the limp was almost gone. He even tried running on it but only for a few steps. 'It won't be long now, Jo,' he said.

'We'll soon have the children away.' Every time Jo asked how many children there were the figure increased.

'We've sent word,' said Widow Horcada. 'Time and again we've told them not to send any more down the line but the children keep coming. There's twelve of them now.'

And suddenly Benjamin was never there any more. For weeks, months, Jo never saw him at the house. Whenever he asked after him Widow Horcada would say he was in the barn with the children, or she would simply pretend not to hear; and when she did that Jo never quite dared to probe any further. He never saw any sign either of the children. Every time he passed the barn he longed to take a look inside; it was so difficult to imagine there were twelve children living in there.

They hardly saw anything of Grandpère these days. He'd leave first thing in the morning. 'Off up to work on the hut,' he'd say. Apparently there was a lot of storm damage, a great hole in the roof and all the shutters had to be replaced. It was the same every morning. 'You'll have to manage the sheep without me,' he'd say. 'I'll be back before dark.'

Hubert was always there to help Jo with the milking. He caught sheep better than anyone Jo knew.

He seemed to understand them, to know which way they were thinking of going. His timing was perfect, stretching out his long arm and catching a back leg with consummate ease.

One morning, with Grandpère gone up to the hut again, the two of them had finished milking the flock and were taking the milk to Jo's mother in the kitchen when they heard a knock on the door. Jo answered it. A German soldier was standing there and there was another behind him.

'Orders of Lieutenant Weissmann,' he said, looking over Jo's shoulder into the house. 'We are searching all the houses.'

'What for?' said Maman coming to the door. Jo wasn't sure if the soldier understood or not for he did not reply.

'*Entschuldigung,*' said the soldier and he walked past them into the kitchen and up the stairs, his boots heavy on the boards above them. There were sounds of furniture being dragged across the floor. Hubert looked alarmed. Maman put a hand on his arm and held it. 'It's all right, Hubert,' she said. 'It's all right. We've got nothing to hide.' The soldier came down the stairs again and went through the kitchen into the barn. Jo followed him. The sheep took fright and packed against the far wall.

'I've got to take the sheep out,' said Jo pushing past the soldier. The soldier shook his head. He clearly did not understand. Jo spoke louder, pointing. 'The sheep, I must put them out. They must eat.' The soldier shrugged his shoulders. Jo had only one thought. Somehow he had to get up to the Widow Horcada's house and warn them. *All* the houses, the soldier had said, they were searching *all* the houses.

The sheep moved infuriatingly slowly out of the village that morning and Rouf was proving even more lethargic than usual. Several times they came to a complete halt bunching tight together in the streets. Only Hubert's loudest whooping managed to shift them and it was some time before the sheep were up in their pastures and grazing. As soon as they were settled Jo left them with Hubert and Rouf and made for Widow Horcada's farm, running. Half-way up the hillside he paused for breath and looked back down towards the village. A soldier on horseback was riding along the road towards where Hubert was sitting on the rock. Lieutenant Weissmann, it had to be – he was the only one who ever rode the horse. There were two soldiers walking along behind him. Jo ducked into the trees, he'd have to keep under cover all the way to the farm. It would take longer but he had no choice. He did not stop again until the back of the house was below him and he was sure he could not be seen from the road below. He raced down across the yard and threw open the door. Widow Horcada was sitting in her chair, her mouth gaping. Her eyes flickered. There was someone behind the door. Jo turned to look. Grandpère was standing there, his arms raised above his head and there was an iron in his hands.

CHAPTER 6

GRANDPÈRE LOWERED THE IRON. 'WHAT THE devil are you doing here, Jo?'

It was a moment or two before Jo could catch his breath. 'They're coming,' he said. 'The soldiers, they're coming this way. They're searching all the houses.'

'You sure?' said Grandpère going to the window.

'I'm sure,' Jo said.

'Well,' said Widow Horcada. 'You told us it would happen, Henri, and it has. It's what we planned for isn't it?'

'You'll be all right will you?' Grandpère said pulling on his coat.

'Of course we will,' she said. 'Now get going and be quick about it.' Grandpère had the back door open by now. 'And Henri, don't come back till we come for you. If we don't come you'll know the worst and you'll know what to do.' Grandpère made to come back into the room. 'No goodbyes,' said Widow Horcada and she waved him away. 'Just go.' And the door closed behind him. 'Come here, Jo,' she said and she took his hand. 'How far away are they?'

'They were down on the road,' said Jo. 'Five minutes, maybe ten, but they could be going further down the valley to Mougin's place or maybe...'

'They'll be here. Sooner or later they'll be here,' said the Widow. 'We'll plan on sooner. Now, everyone knows you go shopping for me?' Jo nodded. 'That's what you've come for then, money for the shopping. Here.' She stood up and took a few coins from the mantlepiece. 'Take it,' she said. 'And you'll be eating when they come. Boys are always eating aren't they? So, fetch a plate and a knife and cut yourself some bread. We'll keep it natural. I'll be knitting, you'll be eating.'

'But what about the children?' asked Jo.

'Just you let me do the worrying,' she said. 'All you've got to do is eat.' And Widow Horcada gathered her stitches and busied herself over her knitting. 'I've done ten of these jumpers now,' she said, 'all sizes.' But Jo wasn't thinking of the children any more.

'Why was Grandpère here?' he said. Widow Horcada did not answer. 'Does he know all about Benjamin, about Anya, about the children?' The Widow looked up from her knitting.

'I didn't want to tell him,' she said. 'He guessed most of it and I had to tell him the rest. He's no fool, your grandfather, not an easy man to lie to – never was. You remember that day you brought him up here? Well, he kept on at me about why I needed the money. He had to know the truth he said or else he wouldn't help me, so I had to tell him.'

'About me too?' said Jo.

'Everything,' she said. 'Now look what you've made me do, I've dropped my stitches again.' She was still trying to gather them when they heard the snorting of a horse outside and the sound of hooves on the cobbles. 'Eat, Jo, eat,' whispered Widow Horcada and Jo stuffed a crust of bread in his mouth and chewed on it. Somehow it helped to control the fear rising in the pit of his stomach. There were voices outside now, a barked command and then the expected knock on the door. Widow Horcada waited for a few moments, put her knitting in her lap and composed herself.

'Come in,' she said, and the door opened.

Lieutenant Weissmann clicked his heels. He was very tall in the room, his head almost touching the beams. 'Pardon Madame,' he said looking around the room, 'but we are carrying out searches.'

'Are you indeed?' said Widow Horcada coldly. 'And what is it that you are searching for, may I ask?'

The Lieutenant smiled. 'We shan't know that, Madame,' he said, 'until we find it, shall we?' He ushered a soldier past him and pointed to the staircase, then he turned his gaze on Jo. 'And what are you doing here?' he asked. Jo found he couldn't speak so he didn't try.

'He does my shopping for me, don't you, Jo?'

'Ah yes,' said Lieutenant Weissmann studying him hard; and he turned again to the Widow. 'You live here alone?'

'Yes,' said Widow Horcada. 'My husband was killed in the last war. I am quite alone.'

'I am sorry, Madame,' said the Lieutenant.

'Sorry? And what is it that you are sorry for Lieutenant? That I am a widow? That I am alone? Or that you are searching my house and treating me like a common criminal? Which?'

'*Entschuldigung* Madame,' said the Lieutenant stiffly, and he called upstairs: '*Etwas*?'

'*Nein Herr Oberleutnant,*' and the soldier's boots were heavy on the staircase as he came back down into the kitchen.

'And what do you keep in your barn, Madame?' said the Lieutenant.

'Animals,' she said, sniffing and wrinkling her nose. 'Farmers usually keep animals in barns, it's what they're for. Before I sold them I used to keep my pigs in there through the Winter.'

'And now?'

'Nothing, some hay for my cow, that's all.'

'Then you won't mind if we take a look?' said Lieutenant Weissmann.

'Lieutenant,' she said. 'Let us not play games with each other. You will search my barn whether I want you to or not.'

'Indeed, Madame, but I only meant...'

Widow Horcada interrupted him. 'I know what you meant. Do it, Lieutenant. Just do what you have to do and leave us in peace.'

'*Auf Wiedersehen* Madame,' he said and they left, shutting the door behind them.

Jo ran to the window. One of the soldiers was pushing at the barn door. He kicked it and it flew open.

'They're going in,' said Jo. 'They'll find them.'

'No they won't, Jo,' said the Widow. 'They won't find anything because there's nothing in there but hay, bracken and a lot of old pigs' muck.'

'Then where are they?' said Jo.

'Come away from that window,' said Widow Horcada smiling. 'And you can put my money back before you forget.' She took his hand as he passed her. 'You're a brave boy, Jo. It's a funny thing you know, but when you're old and used up like I am and there's only the grave to look forward to, nothing seems to frighten you very much.' They heard the barn door shut and the horse moving off. 'We'll wait for an hour or so just to be sure,' she said, 'then we'll go and find them.'

'Where are they?' asked Jo again.

'You'll find out soon enough,' she said.

It was a long silent climb up through the trees. Widow Horcada walked ahead of him, pausing every so often for breath. There must be no talking, she had said, not one word. All the time Jo was trying to guess where the children might be. They were heading up towards the plateau. There were several shepherd's huts up there and some of them would certainly be large enough to house the children. He could not think of anywhere else they might be. Where the mountain met the tree line the trees grew more sparsely. There was more daylight above them now. Jo looked up. A few spindly trees clung for life to the rock face above him. Widow Horcada stopped and leaned on her stick. She looked about her, listening, her finger to her lips; and then she was bending and pulling aside the undergrowth. Behind the bracken and the brambles was a curtain of sacks. She lifted it and beckoned Jo through after her. Jo ducked down and found himself in darkness. She had him by the wrist and was leading him along what seemed to be a passage and Jo was groping ahead of him like a blind man. A single light glowed dimly far ahead of him. Then there were several lights, lights that were suddenly bright and flickering as another curtain of sacks parted in front of them. Grandpère was there, holding out his hand to help him in and Benjamin was beside him. A young girl clung to Benjamin's arm and Jo saw at once that it was Léah. He wasn't sure she even recognised him at first, but then her eyes lit up. 'Jo,' she said, and she took his hand at once as if he belonged to her and led him deeper into the cave.

The cave was narrow, low and long, and dimly lit with guttering lamps hung here and there along the walls. At first glance it was not always easy to distinguish the children from their own shadows. The place smelt of oil and cheese and meadow hay. Everywhere the floor was covered with bracken, except for a great bed of hay in the darkest corner where a huddle of children were curled together in sleep.

Along a winding track in the bracken came a

wooden train propelled towards him by two boys on their knees, one chuffachuffing and the other oo-ooing. Then the wagons became unhitched and there was an instantaneous quarrel. Benjamin crouched down beside them to make thé peace which was achieved as soon as the train was linked together again. Jo recognised it then as his own train, the battered train of his childhood – he hadn't set eyes on it for years. He looked back at Grandpère who smiled and shrugged his shoulders. 'Didn't think you'd mind,' he said. Three girls sat side by side over the same book, the girl in the middle reading aloud to the other two, one of whom turned the page to see for herself what would happen next. The reader snatched her hand back and held on to it for a moment before taking off her glasses and breathing on to them. It was then that she looked up and saw Jo. She froze. Quite suddenly all the children had noticed him. 'Jo,' Léah announced. She was introducing him. 'Jo.' The sleeping ones on the hay were nudged into consciousness. Jo felt the stare of each of them. It was more curiosity than hostility he thought, but there was suspicion enough in those looks to make him feel uncomfortable.

'Well Jo,' said Benjamin. 'What do you think of it? Three months I've been up here now. The children and me, we've made ourselves quite snug. We've got running water at the back of the cave. Your grand-father's idea it was. We've got a lot to thank him for.'

'I used to come up here a lot at one time,' Grandpère said. 'My father, your great-grandfather, Jo – God rest him – he used to do a bit of smuggling over the border – brandy mostly, everyone was at it in those days – and he kept his stuff in here. To tell you the truth I'd almost forgotten about the place until they showed me that barn full of children. If those soldiers had come looking during the Winter ... well, it doesn't bear thinking about does it?'

'Then don't think about it, Henri,' said Widow Horcada lowering herself gingerly on to a wooden bench. 'No sense in thinking about what could have happened especially when it didn't.'

'Maybe, maybe not,' said Grandpère somewhat tersely. 'I'm telling you, Alice, today was a warning. I've told you before we've got to get these children out of here, and soon. I can take them. I know these mountains like the back of my hand.'

'And I've told you before,' said Widow Horcada, 'you've got no patience, never have had. We've got to wait till the time is right. D'you think we want to keep the children here a minute longer than we have to? Do you? Benjamin's ankle may be better and the snow may be gone; but you tell me Henri Lalande, you tell me how we're going to take twelve children past those German patrols. You've seen them, they're everywhere, and anyway there's two or three children still too weak to make the journey.' Grandpère was about to argue. 'No, Henri, they're safer here. You said yourself no one knows this place except you. We bide our time like we all agreed.'

'I was up in the mountains again only yesterday,' said Benjamin, 'looking for a way through. Two, maybe three times a week I'm up there studying the routes the patrols take, how often they come, when they come. I don't care how well you know them, Henri, you'd never make it. On your own maybe, if you're lucky, but not with all these children. We've got to wait. That's all we can do – wait and pray.'

Someone was tugging Jo's coat. He looked down. A small boy gripped his arm and dragged him away.

'That's Michael,' Benjamin called after him. 'He wants you to play chess. You won't stand a chance.'

From his size Jo thought Michael must be about half his age. Michael fell on his knees in the bracken and set out the pieces on a flat rock that served as a chessboard. The squares were marked out with white chalk. He held out his clenched fists and Jo knelt down and tapped his right hand. Black. Jo was happy. He always won with black. Jo was good at chess, so good

Laurent wouldn't play him any more, nor would Grandpère. Only Monsieur Audap beat him regularly. Suddenly he was aware of shadows crowding in around him; all the other children were coming to watch. Michael never looked up at him once during the game. In between moves he sat with his arms folded, his eyes on the board, and when it was his turn he moved his piece without hesitation and without any apparent thought. After half a dozen moves Jo just wished it to be over. Every piece he lost provoked a sigh of pleasure from the audience and when a few minutes later Jo found himself checkmate, Michael looked up for the first time and smiled. Jo saw that when he smiled his ears moved and he could not help but smile back.

'You play better than your grandfather,' said Michael. 'I beat him in ten moves.'

It was little enough consolation for Jo as he went back down through the trees with Grandpère later that day. Grandpère was grumbling. 'She always argues, that woman. Trouble is she's always right too, and that only makes it worse. It's true enough what she says. There's patrols out everywhere, along the river, in the woods. Once up the top you could maybe slip past on a dark night; but between here and there you'd never do it, not with the children.

There's got to be a way through, there's got to be.'

'Grandpère,' said Jo. 'Why didn't you tell me?'

'Tell you what?'

'You've been going up there all the time haven't you? Why didn't you tell me?'

Grandpère stopped and turned to him. 'Because she told me not to, Jo. And she's right. It's safer not to know. Come to that, I could ask the same of you. You never told me, did you?'

'Same reason,' said Jo.

'There you are then,' said Grandpère and he smiled. 'I'm proud of what you've done, Jo, and Maman would be too; but not a word at home, Jo, not even a look. We don't talk about it at all. Not behind closed doors, not with a hundred bleating sheep around us. I don't want her knowing, Jo. You know how she worries.'

They walked on for a bit. 'That little boy, that Michael,' said Jo. 'He said he beat you in ten moves.'

'So he did,' said Grandpère, 'but he's hardly a little boy. Benjamin says he's nearly fifteen – same sort of age as you. Nothing much of him is there? That's what hunger does for you.'

The Germans found nothing in the village that day except for a couple of unusable rifles. For some weeks afterwards there was a frosty enmity between the villagers and the soldiers. Hubert blew his raspberries again and Laurent put his tongue out at them – when they weren't looking of course. Even Armand Jollet stopped opening doors for them. But time healed the wound and everyone was soon back on speaking terms again with the soldiers. There was a greater caution now and a new understanding, that harmless though they might seem, the soldiers were still the enemy and when called upon, they would behave like it.

Jo avoided all of them now, even the Corporal. Every time he saw them he could not put it out of his mind that these men were hunters. They were hunting down Benjamin and Léah, Michael and the others. Just to look at the soldiers made him feel uncomfortable; so he distanced himself from them, he accepted no sweets and exchanged no civilities.

At home, too, Jo felt uncomfortable. He had lived for a long time now with his secret and up till now had felt no sense of guilt at keeping it from Maman. But now that his secret had become a kind of conspiracy with Grandpère he found himself acting out a charade. It was hateful for him to have to lie to her, to watch her being constantly and successfully deceived. He found it more and more difficult to look her in the eye, to talk to her even, so he spent all the hours he could out with Rouf and Hubert looking after the sheep.

He was sitting on his rock with Hubert one morning

when he saw the Corporal coming along the road. He had no rifle, only binoculars round his neck. He stopped and smoothed Rouf who did not discriminate at all – he liked anyone who adored him, Germans included.

'It's Friday,' the Corporal announced. 'On Fridays I have some hours off duty and I do not forget my promise.'

'Promise?' said Jo.

'The eagle, the binoculars. You don't remember?' Hubert was inspecting the binoculars closely. 'You want to look, Hubert?' said the Corporal. 'I show you.' And he took off the binoculars and hung them around Hubert's neck. Hubert held them to his eyes and looked out across the valley. The Corporal tapped him on the shoulder and pointed upward. A lark hovered there noisily. A moment or two later Hubert found it in the binoculars and the Corporal focused it for him. Hubert roared with excitement. The Corporal laughed and patted him on the back.

'Well, Jo,' he said, 'do you want to come with me?'

'Take Hubert,' said Jo and he looked away.

'As you wish,' said the Corporal quietly, and he turned to Hubert. 'You come with me, Hubert?' and pointed towards the mountains. 'We look for eagles, yes?' He held his arms out wide. 'Eagles, high up.' He made binoculars out of his hands, put them to his eyes and scanned the mountains. 'Eagles,' he said flapping his arms. 'You come?' Hubert looked at Jo and then at the sheep.

'Go on,' said Jo. 'I'll mind them.' Rouf got up to go with them but Jo held him back; he needed the company.

He sat with his thoughts all that morning. He'd been up to the cave several times now with Grandpère and Widow Horcada, carrying oil and food, and each time he'd wondered at Benjamin's seemingly unshakeable optimism. The more he thought about it the more he could see no good reason for it. The days passed, the months passed and still Anya did not come. If she was alive after all this time – and like Widow Horcada Jo found that increasingly difficult to believe – then where was she and why hadn't she come? He never shared his misgivings with Benjamin, for in Benjamin's few unguarded moments Jo sensed a fragility in his faith that might not stand the test of reason. And besides, it was easier and more comforting to go along with Benjamin's repeated assurances. 'She'll be hiding up somewhere,' he'd said. 'Maybe in a barn, maybe in a cave just like ours. She'll come. God willing, she'll come. God looks after his own, Jo. He always does.' Jo hoped hard that he did.

News of the war was better. The Germans were being driven back out of Russia and out of Africa, but liberation was still a distant dream and a dream no one dared talk of for fear that it still might not happen. Yet Jo could see no other hope for the children or for Benjamin. The patrols were just as frequent and watchful as ever; there always seemed to be some children sick and Benjamin would not hear of leaving any of them behind. 'We all go or we none of us go,' he said. 'Wait and pray. Our time will come.'

Jo would have liked to have made friends with the children in the cave. They all knew who he was by now but they still treated him like a stranger and hid themselves behind their dark eyes – all except Michael who never let him leave without beating him at chess. Michael had recently become one of the sick children. He had developed an abscess on his leg and a fever with it but It didn't stop him wiping Jo off the board every time in under twenty moves. The games were always held in complete silence, a rapt audience all around. Jo still chose black, believing and hoping that one day it would bring him luck, but it never did him any good. Widow Horcada would never let him stay very long after the game so there was not much time for talking, and when they did Michael was full of questions about Jo, about his family, about the animals on the farm, about his school. He would say little about himself, only that he could speak four languages, Polish, French, German and a little English. 'I want to speak ten,' he said. But he never once spoke of his family. Jo asked Widow Horcada where they all were and she would not tell him. 'There's some things better not to think about,' she said and nothing more was said about it; and Grandpère was no more forthcoming. Either they didn't know or they didn't want to talk about it, Jo was not sure which. But the more he thought about it the more he was convinced that they did know and that they were just not telling him. He wondered why. The sun was hot on his head and Jo felt like lying down, but he'd done that once before and he would never do it again. He talked to Rouf instead.

Some hours later, as he was moving the sheep further down the valley to fresh pastures, he saw the Corporal and Hubert walking across the field towards him. Hubert broke into a leaping run, shouting through the sheep as he came. The sheep scattered in all directions, their bells jangling. From the wild gesticulations and excited gruntings it became clear very quickly that Jo had missed something special. The Corporal confirmed it.

'It was a big one,' he said. 'I have never seen an eagle so big. He saw it first, didn't you, Hubert?' Hubert had the binoculars to his eyes and was pointing to the mountains. 'And I did not believe him,' the Corporal went on, 'not at first, because I could not see it. It was not in the air you see; it was on the ground. Perhaps it had just caught something, maybe it was a rabbit; and then it took off up into the air and we followed it.' He laughed. 'Hubert would not take the binoculars from his eyes and he kept tripping over, but we did not lose it. We followed it higher always higher, until it landed on a shelf of rock. And there were twigs there, I saw them. I think it must be a nest Jo.'

'Did you see any young birds?' Jo said.

The Corporal shook his head. 'Maybe we go back another day. Next Friday yes?'

'Maybe,' said Jo, shrugging his shoulders. He was doing his best to conceal his enthusiasm.

'Good,' said the Corporal. 'I shall look forward to it.'

Even after he had gone Hubert never stopped flying about like an eagle. As they drove the sheep back into the village that evening he was still at it, flapping his arms like wings, curling his hands into claws and shrieking. Jo found himself almost annoyed with Hubert for having enjoyed it so much. Eagle's nest or not, he would not go with the Corporal next Friday, he would not.

That Sunday after Mass Jo saw Father Lasalle talking earnestly to Grandpère and Lieutenant Weissmann outside the church door. At lunch Grandpère was unusually quiet – Maman noticed it too.

'Is there something the matter?' she said.

Grandpère pushed away his plate and lit a cigarette. 'That Boche Corporal, the big one,' he said, 'you know him? Well, he's just about the best of them I'd say.'

'What about him?' said Maman.

'He had three daughters,' Grandpère said, 'and now he's got two. One of them was killed in a bombing raid on Berlin last week.'

'Poor man,' said Maman. 'Poor man.'

Grandpère stood up, angry. 'Why poor man, eh? If he'd stayed at home and looked after his family like he should have done, like they all should have done, he'd still have three daughters, wouldn't he? And my son, your husband, wouldn't be shut up in some camp, and those children...' He stopped short and coughed.

Maman looked at him sharply. 'What children?' she asked, but Grandpère pretended not to have heard and by the time she asked again he was almost out of the room.

'I'm going up to the hut,' he said and he was gone.

'Why is Grandpère angry?' asked Christine.

'I don't know, dear,' said Maman still frowning after him. 'I don't know.'

The following Friday the mist was still lying in the valley when the Corporal came by as he'd promised he would. Jo half hoped that he wouldn't come for he knew that he would not be able to refuse him now, and that's how it turned out. The Corporal seemed a different man. All the jollity was gone, all the warmth. His eyes were red and vacant. 'You are coming, Jo?' he said, and he handed Jo the binoculars. Hubert wanted to come again but he was quite used to taking turns, and anyway the half bar of chocolate the Corporal offered seemed a tempting enough substitute. They left him guarding the sheep. When Jo looked back he was making Rouf lie down and beg for his chocolate.

They walked on without speaking. 'We won't be able to see much in the mist,' said Jo.

'When we get higher it will be better.'

It was several minutes before Jo found the courage to speak of it but he knew he had to. 'About what happened to your daughter,' he said. 'I'm sorry, everyone's sorry.'

'Thank you, Jo,' said the Corporal. 'Thank you.' And then he started talking and once he had started he didn't stop. 'If there has to be a war,' he said, 'then it should be fought between soldiers. Before, it was always between soldiers, that I can understand. I do not like it, but I can understand it. At Verdun it was one soldier in a uniform against another soldier in another uniform. What have women and children to do with the fighting of wars, tell me that? Every day since I hear about my daughter, every day I ask myself many questions and I try to answer them. It is not so easy. What are we doing here, Wilhelm, I ask myself? Answer: I'm guarding the frontier. Question: why? Answer: to stop people escaping. Question: why do they want to escape? Answer: because they are in fear of their lives. Question: who are these people? Answer: Frenchmen who do not want to be taken to work in Germany, maybe a few prisoners-of-war escaping, and Jews. Question: who is it that threatens the lives of Jews? Answer: we do. Question: why? Answer: there is no answer. Question: and when they are captured, what happens? Answer: concentration camp. Question: and then? Answer: no answer, not because there is no answer, Jo, but because we are frightened to know the answer.' He wiped his cheeks with the back of his hand and laughed. 'You see what happens when you ask so many questions, Jo? When I was little I always asked too many questions and my mother would become impatient. When I asked why again and again she would say, "a blue reason, Willi, a blue reason".' Jo smiled at that. 'So,' said the Corporal, 'we smile again. We must smile. It is good to smile. Now we look for eagles.'

As they climbed out of the trees they left the mist below them and reached a wide plain of spongy grass, dotted with grey-blue thistles and scattered rocks, with a silver stream running through it.

'It was here,' said the Corporal. 'We were here when we saw it last time.' He pointed upwards. 'Look, can you see there? Up there, half-way up the mountain. How do you say it, a ledge, yes? It was up there, I am sure of it.' Jo trained the binoculars on the rock face. 'Higher, a little higher, Jo. Can you see it?' And there it was, a wide ledge of rock, a dark recess behind it and at one end a nest of twigs, but no eagle.

'She's not there,' said Jo, 'and I can't see a chick.'

'She'll come,' said the Corporal, 'if she comes once then she'll come again. We must be patient. We will move higher up the mountain, that way we can see better.'

Jo followed him across the valley, leapt the stream and scrambled up the shale on hands and feet until they came to a steep slope that was always covered in blueberries in September. Jo had often been up there picking them with Papa. They squatted down in the shadow of a great rock. From there they could look back across the narrow valley and into the ledge.

The Corporal took the binoculars and trained them. 'Better,' he said, 'much better. Here she will not see us, but we will see her. Now we wait, we wait and pray.' Jo looked at him. 'Something is wrong?' asked the Corporal.

Jo turned away and shook his head. 'I know someone else who often says the same thing,' said Jo, 'that's all.'

'Here,' said the Corporal, 'you have the binoculars. Now we must be still. We must be silent.'

They sat side by side, knees drawn up, eyes scanning the sky about them. They spotted birds by the score, vultures, ravens, larks, buzzards and a lone red kite that absorbed them for an hour or more, but no eagle. Jo was training the binoculars on a vulture high above him, drawing it into focus until it filled the circle of the glass. He could see the feathers on it, how they wrapped around the wind and kept it floating up there. Suddenly the Corporal's arm was on his shoulder and squeezing him. Jo swung the glasses across to the ledge and caught up with the eagle just as she landed. She dropped something at her feet, Jo could not make out what it was. The eagle shook herself and surveyed the world beneath her, then she picked up her prey – it looked like a marmot Jo thought – and sidled along the ledge towards the nest. There she dropped it, stood a claw on it and began to pick at it. It was then that Jo saw something moving in the shadows under the rock behind her. A chick came lurching and hopping over the twigs towards the eagle.

'Look,' he whispered. 'Look.'

'Please?' said the Corporal holding out his hand, and Jo handed him the binoculars. *'Prima! Ausgezeichnet!'* murmured the Corporal. *'Ausgezeichnet.* I think there's two of them, Jo. Yes, there's two,' and he handed the binoculars back to Jo. Infuriatingly it took some time for Jo to find the ledge again and focus; but then he had them, all three of them, and he was watching an eagles' tea party of shredded marmot. They pulled at it, all of them, tearing at the same piece and hopping backwards until it snapped. Jo felt the Corporal tapping him on his arm but he was so entranced that he was reluctant to hand back the glasses. The tapping became more insistent. Jo lowered the glasses and made to hand them over but the Corporal didn't seem to want them. He was pointing down to the valley below them. Jo looked. Three soldiers were moving slowly towards the stream. He could hear their voices now. Jo turned his binoculars on them but before he could focus they had moved out of sight behind a large boulder. One by one they emerged the other side. Jo looked up at the Corporal who shrugged his shoulders and smiled. 'It's all right, Jo,' he said, 'I've got my papers.' Jo looked down at them again. Someone was moving through the trees beyond the boulder. Another soldier, Jo thought. He lifted the binoculars a fraction; it was no soldier. As Jo focused the binoculars his worst fears were realised. Benjamin was crouching now at the edge of the wood. He was looking this way and that, as if he was about to dash out across the open towards the cover of some nearby rocks, and Jo saw with a sickening heart that from where Benjamin was he could not possibly see the patrol behind the boulder. They only had to walk on a few more paces and he would come face to face with them.

CHAPTER 7

THE CORPORAL WAS ON HIS FEET, HANDS CUPPED to his mouth. 'Ola! Ola!' he shouted, and the echo resounded around the valley. The patrol stopped. 'Ola! Ola!' and he waved both arms in the air. The soldiers were looking about them in alarm, their rifles at the ready. The Corporal laughed and shook his head. 'I think it is Rudi's patrol,' he said. 'We call them "the grandfathers". They are even older than I am.' Jo looked beyond the boulder into the trees. Benjamin had vanished. One of the soldiers had seen them now and was pointing excitedly. 'Maybe we should go down to them,' said the Corporal, 'so that they can see who we are. We do not want them to think that we are escaping over the border, do we? Come on, Jo.' And he helped him to his feet. The soldiers were running up towards them. 'It's Rudi. No one else runs like Rudi. You know what he is, Jo? He's, how do you say, a taxidermist. You know what they do? No? I tell you then. He is someone who stuffs dead animals, fish perhaps, birds even.' Jo was not listening. He was straining to find some movement amongst the trees beyond the boulder. There was none. Benjamin had gone. He was sure of it now. He was safe. Jo heard his heart pounding in his throat and swallowed to stop it. '*Was ist los?*' said the Corporal. 'Something is wrong, Jo?' Jo shook his head. 'You don't look so good.'

'I'm all right,' said Jo. 'I'm all right.' The Corporal took Jo by the elbow. 'Come, we go down. Poor old Rudi, it would give him a heart attack if we made him come all the way up here.'

There followed a laughing reunion half-way up the slope. Jo could not understand much of what they were saying but he could see that the Corporal was explaining all about the eagle's nest and by the way they looked at him all about Jo too. There was lots of nodding, lots of '*ja ja*'s and more laughing, and then as if to prove the point the eagle shrieked right above them, circled once and soared away over the peaks, the soldiers' binoculars trained on her. But Jo's eyes were still searching the trees. 'Quick Jo,' said the Corporal, 'you will miss it.' But in the time Jo took to lift the binoculars to his eyes and focus, the eagle had gone and the sky above the peaks was empty.

It was late afternoon before they rounded the bend in the track and saw Hubert sitting where they had left him on his rock. Rouf lifted his head off his lap and yawned. He stretched and came plodding towards them. Hubert didn't hear them until the sheep moved in closer together, then he turned and saw them. He was clearly more pleased to see the binoculars than anything else. In a trice he had them around his neck. The Corporal smiled and began to walk away.

'What about your binoculars?' Jo called after him.

He walked backwards for a few paces as he spoke. 'He can keep them. They make him happy, yes? And I have another pair, my army ones, much better, much stronger. Those are my own, yours now, Hubert. *Auf Wiedersehen.'*

It took some time for Hubert to believe that the binoculars were really his but when he did everyone in the village had to know and everyone had to look through them and share in his joy. He wore them around his neck constantly, even when he was milking the sheep. His father said he often slept with them on at night.

More than ever now the Corporal was held in

genuine affection throughout the village, for the gift did not smack of bribery but of open generosity. His spirits seemed to recover quickly in this cocoon of warmth – perhaps a little too quickly some said, Madame Soulet for one; but Jo knew this not to be so.

The two of them, the Corporal and Jo, often sat for long hours together on the rock. They were not allowed up into the mountains again the Corporal told him – Lieutenant Weissmann had forbidden it. But anyway they were content to be where they were. They watched the sheep and the birds, and Jo felt the raw pain of grief in the Corporal's long silences. The Corporal never again spoke of his dead daughter, except once when he said it would be her birthday soon. It was that day that Hubert came stumbling along the track towards them, his binoculars around his neck as usual. He seemed unusually awkward and shy as he sat down beside Jo and rocked back and forth. He often seemed to do this when he was tense. Quite suddenly he stopped rocking and took a deep breath. He reached inside his shirt. Jo had expected him to produce a frog or a toad perhaps, but when his hand came out he was holding a packet of cigarettes. He reached across Jo and offered one to the Corporal.

The Corporal shook his head and smiled. 'No thank you, Hubert. Since the war began I smoke too much. In my letters I promise my wife not to smoke. If I promise then I can stop, you understand me, yes?' Hubert frowned and insisted, holding the packet closer to the Corporal. 'Very well, Hubert, just this once then,' he said, and he took the packet.

Hubert drew his knees up and rocked again. The Corporal opened the packet and when Jo saw the cotton wool he knew what it was all about. Hubert had his hands over his eyes as the Corporal tugged gently at the cotton wool until it came free. He seemed to guess now what it was and pulled away the cotton wool with the utmost care. It was a tiny white chalice, and as the Corporal turned it slowly in his hand on the bed of cotton wool Jo could see that around it flew two golden eagles, their spread wings touching.

'He makes them,' said Jo.

The Corporal nodded. 'I know,' he said, holding it up to the light. It was translucent. 'Hubert's father,' he went on, 'he showed me his collection.' He folded it in the cotton wool again and slipped it back inside the cigarette packet. He slipped down off the rock and stood in front of Hubert. He reached out and took Hubert's hands away from his face. He leaned forward and kissed Hubert on both cheeks, patted him on the knee and walked away.

'He liked it,' said Jo, but Hubert had spotted a

limping sheep and was off after it, shadowing it with Rouf into a corner of the field until they had it boxed in. He caught it by the back leg, picked something out of the foot, smacked its bottom and sent it bleating on its way.

They brought the sheep back in early that day because it was coming on to rain. Everyone else had the same idea so there was a muddle of sheep in the narrow village streets before they managed to drive them at last into the walled yard in front of the house. Jo thought he was a few sheep short and was counting them when Grandpère came to the door and called him in. Something was up, he could see it in his face. The sheep moved aside as he walked through them. Grandpère stood on the doorstep, a cigarette hanging between his lips.

'Is it the children?' Jo spoke softly.

'Nothing like that,' said Grandpère throwing away his cigarette. 'Indoors, I've got something to show you.'

'What about the milking?'

'The sheep can wait, Jo,' he said. 'Come on,' and he took his arm.

As Jo went into the kitchen his suspicions were confirmed. Something wrong. Christine was sitting silently on her mother's lap. Christine never sat on anyone's lap and was never quiet. She was staring across the room. Maman rested her chin on Christine's head. There were tears in her eyes. 'Jo,' she said, and then Jo saw the man standing by the window. The stranger had his back to him, his hands deep in the pockets of a long, dirty coat. As he turned round the evening light fell across his face and Jo saw at once it was his father. It was not the father he remembered from nearly four years before, but a smaller man, a thinner man, whose hair was no longer black but quite grey, and when Jo hugged him he could feel the sharp shoulder blades through his coat.

'Let me look at you, Jo,' said Papa, and he held him at arm's length. 'You've grown,' he said. The skin was stretched like paper over his cheekbones. 'Not that bad is it, Jo? You do recognise me, don't you?'

'Of course, Papa,' said Jo.

'More than your sister did. Still, that's not her fault is it? She was no more than a babe when I left.'

'They let him out, Jo,' said Grandpère. 'Sent him home.'

'Don't go thinking it was out of the kindness of their hearts,' said Papa. 'They'd had all of me they wanted, used me all up.' Jo turned to his mother for an explanation.

'Papa's sick, Jo. Tuberculosis,' she said. 'They sent

him home because he couldn't work any more.'

'It was the damp,' said Papa. 'There were dozens of us like it. No use to them any more. So they sent us home. You know Michel, Michel Maurois? They sent us back together, him and me. He's not grumbling, and neither am I, I can tell you. What's a bit of a wheezy chest when it's a passport home. Just give me a week or two and I'll be right as rain.'

They sat long together over supper that evening while Papa tried to catch up on the years he'd missed, and as the hours passed Christine ventured closer and closer to him. By the time she was taken up to bed she let him kiss her goodnight.

'That's the best thing that's happened to me in a long time,' he said.

Grandpère tried to ask about the prison camp but Papa would say nothing about it except to say that 'you learn things about yourself you never wanted to know'. There were long silences when he seemed to drift away into a world of his own. A mere mention of the soldiers in the village made him immediately angry and even the subject of Grandpère's pigs seemed to irritate him. Until he asked after the sheep Maman had said very little.

'Jo stepped right into your shoes,' she said, and Jo saw Papa's face darken suddenly. 'I told you in my letters, didn't I?' she went on. 'You'd have been proud of him. Maybe he missed school more often than he should but Monsieur Audap understood. Thinks very highly of our Jo does Monsieur Audap.'

'Monsieur Audap?' said Papa.

'His teacher,' she said. 'Don't you remember?'

'Oh yes,' said Papa and he looked away. He seemed to have forgotten so much about the village, about everything, and Jo could see that it hurt him to know it and to know that others knew it. Jo wished Maman would stop talking about how useful he'd been. Every word she spoke seemed to shrivel Papa up, but still she went on. 'Hubert helped him of course. We couldn't have managed without him. You remember Hubert?'

'Of course,' Papa snapped. 'Of course I do.'

Grandpère tried to make light of it. 'And me,' he said. 'What about me? Did I sit on my backside for four years, eh? Who took the sheep up on to the summer pastures? I did. Who moved the sheep when he was at school, eh? I did. Your old father, that's who.' He got up and poured Papa some more wine. 'And now you're back again I can hang up my boots.'

'Not yet you can't,' said Maman. 'We've got to get him well first. Good food and a warm house and plenty of rest. That's what he needs.'

'Don't fuss me,' said Papa, and he drank down his

wine as if he hated it.

Grandpère leaned forward and tapped his knee. 'I've been courting, son,' he said, and Papa's laughter filled the house for the first time.

'It's true,' said Maman, 'everyone knows it. He's up and down to that old woman's house. Talk of the village it is.'

'What old woman?' Papa asked.

'Widow Horcada,' said Maman, 'the Black Widow.'

'You're not serious?' Papa was still laughing.

'And why not?' said Grandpère in mock indignation. 'Cleverest woman in the parish. She never parts with a penny she doesn't have to. She even pays Jo with honey doesn't she Jo?'

'What for?'

'For carrying her shopping,' said Grandpère.

Jo sat in silent admiration. In a few moments he had cheered Papa and explained in advance all the comings and goings to and from the Widow Horcada's house. Papa was still chuckling as he got up.

'I can see I came back just in time to stop my father from making an old fool of himself.'

'Too late for that, son,' he said. 'I'm a smitten man and there's nothing you nor anyone can do about it.'

Papa was putting on his coat.

'Where are you going?' Maman said.

'Out,' he said. 'You know, whilst I was in the camp I looked forward to a lot of things, to seeing you, to being home again.' He frowned suddenly. 'You won't believe this,' he said, 'but sometimes I even forgot what you all looked like, all except Rouf there. And you can't look forward to what you can't remember. What I wanted to do most was to walk the hills at night, to feel alive again, to feel free. So that's what I'm going to do.'

They looked at each other frantically as he walked towards the door. 'But you can't,' said Maman. 'You're tired. You're not well. You'll catch a chill.'

'I'll be all right,' he said, opening the door. 'I won't be long.'

Grandpère was beside him. He took his arm and shut the door firmly. 'You can't go out,' he said. 'There's a curfew.'

'Curfew?'

'After nine thirty. If the Boche catch you outside after nine thirty...'

'What'll they do?' said Papa, the fury rising in his voice. 'Put me in prison? Shoot me? Let them. I've been shut up for four years and now I'm home I'm not letting any Boche make a prisoner of me in my own home. I'll come and I'll go as I please. Now out of my way, Papa. Out of my way!' Grandpère stood aside and Papa opened the door, pulled up his collar and walked out into the darkness.

They sat up and waited for him, dreading the sound of running boots, of shouting voices or even a volley of shots. The longer they waited the more terrible their fears became. When he did come back an hour or so later, all he said was: 'I saw them but they didn't see me.' The walk seemed to have dissipated the anger in him.

Jo lay in bed and listened to the murmur of voices from his parents' room next door. Papa really was back home. The last few hours had been no dream. Then came the coughing, fits of coughing followed by silences long enough to let Jo drift into sleep before the next fit began. But the coughing woke Christine and she was up and down the passage all night. Jo gave up all attempts to sleep and waited for the first sound of the dawn chorus.

The next day the village was alive with new joy and hope. No one doubted that the war was being won; it was only a question of time now, that was all. Two of their sons had been returned to them, good enough cause for celebration. In such times any excuse for celebration was seized upon eagerly. Hubert was sent beating his drum around the village, his binoculars still around his neck, and everyone gathered in the Square to hear the Mayor's formal welcome. Papa and Michel Maurois stood either side of him, but Jo thought they endured rather than enjoyed the speech. It finished with a typical flourish. 'We await the day,' said Monsieur Sarthol, 'and it will surely not now be long, when the rest of our fathers and brothers, our uncles and nephews are returned to us once again. *Vive la France*!' Jo looked about him as everyone clapped and cheered and laughed – there wasn't a soldier in sight.

When Jo arrived at school the next morning they crowded around him to congratulate him. He was not sure what he had done to deserve it all, but he enjoyed it just the same. Not everyone, though, wanted to share in the general rejoicing. There were baleful, even resentful looks from across the playground, reminding Jo that many of the children still had fathers in prisoner-of-war camps. Laurent seemed to bear him no grudge, but then Laurent was not like that, and besides he had his reasons. 'I can't stand my father anyway,' he said, 'and neither can my mother. The longer they keep him there the better.' Laurent always said exactly what he thought however it reflected on him, and Jo admired that in him; but now it made Jo feel even more of a fraud. Papa was back home and Jo wished he wasn't. That was the truth of it. No matter how hard he tried to feel differently, he could not. Papa was a stranger to him and not a particularly welcome one either. It wasn't that he hated him, he just did not know him any more.

On Sunday Father Lasalle played a thundering triumphal march on the organ, and thanked God for their deliverance. That evening Jo was in the café when Papa and Michel got up and danced together on the table. The dancing spread out into the Square. Monsieur Audap sang songs nobody thought he ought to know and Hubert wrapped himself in the bearskin from the wall and ran growling and roaring after the children through the streets.

When the Corporal and two other soldiers walked into the café no one took a blind bit of notice. The Corporal nodded and smiled at Jo as he sat down at the table in the corner. Jo smiled back. Suddenly Papa was on his feet, kicking his chair back against the wall. The awful silence was punctuated by distant roars and shrieks out in the Square. Michel tried to hold him back but Papa would not be stopped. He shook himself free, glaring at the three soldiers.

Grandpère stood up beside him. 'Let's go home,' he said.

'Not just yet,' said Papa, and then in a loud voice, 'Well, well. Look what's come to welcome us home, Michel.' He picked up a bottle and walked across the room towards where the soldiers were sitting. '*Guten*

Abend,' he said, the sneer quite evident in his tone.

'Good evening,' said the Corporal without looking up.

'You must join our little party,' said Papa, his voice heavy and slurred with drink. He poured wine into each of their glasses.

Grandpère was trying to pull him away. 'That's enough,' he said. 'Come on, come home.' But Papa ignored him.

'There,' he said, 'some good French wine.' He raised the bottle in the air. 'To victory,' he said.

The soldiers sat, heads bowed, motionless. Then the Corporal stood up and he faced Papa, his glass in his hand. 'I drink to peace,' he said and he drank down his glass and put it on the table.

At that moment Hubert appeared at the door, the bearskin draped over his head and Laurent clutching an arm. Hubert beamed at the Corporal. Papa reached out and caught the swinging binoculars around Hubert's neck. 'Nice,' he said. Hubert laughed and put them to his eyes. He scanned the room until he focused on a stuffed buzzard on a shelf above the bar. He pointed at it. 'Bang!' he said. 'Bang! Bang!' and he laughed and then everyone laughed and was glad of it.

'They're his,' said Laurent. 'The Corporal gave them to you, didn't he, Hubert? You can see anything. I've seen the mountains on the moon.'

'Have you?' said Papa acidly. 'So now we accept presents from them do we?' Jo ran over to him. He had to explain. Papa had to know about the Corporal, about how kind he had been, about what happened to his daughter.

'Papa,' he said, touching his arm.

Papa turned on him, eyes full of fury. 'So he's a friend of yours too, is he?' Jo backed away.

The Corporal picked up his cap from the table. 'Good night,' he said and he passed Hubert on the way out putting a hand on his shoulder. The two soldiers followed him. Papa began to cough violently until he was doubled up. Grandpère took the bottle out of his hand and put an arm around him.

'We'll get him home, Jo,' he said.

In the weeks that followed Papa took very little interest in the farm or in anything else much. He tramped the hillsides all day to return each evening grim and sullen. The evenings he would spend with Michel in the café and Grandpère would go with him to be sure of getting him back before curfew, and when he did come back he was always drunk. Jo remembered him coming home drunk before he went away to the war but then he'd come back happy with the world and singing, now he would sit by the stove and brood darkly. Jo did not even dare to catch his eye for fear of encountering the look of accusing disapproval that he felt was following him wherever he went. The father he'd grown up with, with whom he'd shared the shepherd's hut all summer long, was not the man now sharing his house. They had a stranger living with them and all of them knew it.

Once Jo had come home to find Maman crying in the kitchen. Jo put his arms around her but could not find the words to comfort her. Grandpère did better. 'He'll come out of it, Lise,' he said, 'you'll see. You've got to put yourself in his place. It's like he's come back from the dead – that's what it's like for him. He comes back home expecting everything to be the same and it isn't. You're not the same. I'm not the same. Jo here has grown as tall as he is. There's a lot of bitterness in him, Lise, a lot of poison; but it'll come to a head and then he'll be free of it. Just give him time.' But time seemed only to make matters worse. Even Grandpère's valiant efforts to cheer him fell on deaf ears.

For both of them the journeys up to the children's cave with supplies brought welcome relief. Jo would often go off into the forest with Benjamin to gather firewood. They would talk of the bear and wonder together how big it must be by now and where it was living. And Grandpère would tell his troubles to Widow

Horcada who never seemed that sympathetic.

One afternoon they were on their way back home from the cave when Hubert came running up to them pointing behind him into the bracken and grunting with excitement. He took off his binoculars and handed them to Jo. All Jo could see at first was Rouf's tail, and then a wild boar charged out of the bracken and across the field. Hubert went galloping after him. The last they saw of him he was bounding into the bracken, a stick in his hand, and shouting 'Bang! Bang!' They laughed and turned for home.

Papa was sitting alone in the kitchen. He looked up as they came in. He had a glass of wine in his hand. 'Where've you been?' he said. A frown came across his face as he caught sight of the binoculars. He stood up and lunged for Jo, catching him by the straps of the binoculars. 'What's this then?' Until that moment Jo had forgotten he still had them.

'Hubert's binoculars, Papa. He lent them to me. We saw this boar, didn't we Grandpère?'

'I've been hearing things I don't like, Jo,' said Papa, pulling him closer. Jo could smell the drink on his breath. He tried to pull away but found himself held fast.

'Leave him be,' said Grandpère.

'You stay out of this,' said Papa. 'He's my son. You

and her, you've done enough harm as it is. Only four years I've been gone and look what you've turned him into.'

'What do you mean, Papa?' said Jo.

'Collaborator, that's what I mean.' Jo shook his head. 'I've been told so don't you go denying it. You went off with that Boche Corporal didn't you?'

'I was only watching the eagles.'

'Damn you! Don't lie to me!' The blow came without warning and sent Jo reeling backwards into Grandpère who staggered but held him upright. Jo put his hand on his cheek. He could not feel it. He licked his lip and tasted blood. Grandpère stepped in front of him as Maman came running in. She rushed over to him.

'What've you done?' she cried.

Grandpère sat Jo down in a chair. 'He'll be all right,' he said.

'How could you?' she said. 'He's your own son. What's happened to you? What did they do to you in that camp?'

'You want to know what happened?' Papa was breathing hard. 'I'll tell you what happened. They gutted me like a fish. Don't you understand? They took away four years of my life that's what they did. And when I come back, what do I find, eh? The whole lousy village playing lovey-dovey with them and my own son making friends with the filthy Boche. That's what they are, don't you know what they are? Don't you know what they've done?'

'We had to live,' said Maman reaching for his hand and holding on to it when he tried to pull away from her.

He was crying openly now. 'My own son a collaborator. Do you know what those binoculars are? They're a badge of shame. Hubert's a halfwit. You can't blame him; but my son, my own son...' And he could say no more.

Grandpère pulled a handkerchief out of his pocket and gave it to Jo. 'Here,' he said, 'we don't want blood everywhere do we?' He knocked a cigarette out of a packet and offered one to Papa who shook his head. 'Sit him down, Lise,' said Grandpère firmly, 'and give him a brandy.' She led Papa to a chair. 'And I'll have one too. We'll all have one, to celebrate. You don't know what we're celebrating do you? Well, I'll tell you, but you won't like it. I haven't talked to you like this since you were a little boy and I shouldn't be doing it now in front of Jo, but I'm going to do it anyway.' Grandpère took his brandy. 'Sit down, Lise. You'd better hear this too. You won't like it much either but for a different reason perhaps. Let me tell you something about this boy of yours, this "collaborator" as you call him.'

Jo knew what he was going to say. 'Don't Grand-père,' he said. 'You mustn't.'

'Yes I must, Jo,' he said. 'I'll not have him thinking of you like that, nor of me, nor of any of us.' He turned back to Papa. 'This boy of yours may not look like much, doesn't make a lot of noise, he just goes on quietly; but I'll tell you something for nothing. Single-handed, until just a few months back, single-handed mind you, this boy has been taking Widow Horcada's supplies up and down the mountain. Not much in that, you'd say; but do you know who it's really all been for? Well, I'll tell you then. There's twelve children – Jews – hiding away in a cave up in the forest, waiting to be taken over into Spain. Some of them have been waiting for near enough two years, and all that time they've needed feeding and all that time your Jo's been doing it. Without that boy of yours, that "collaborator", they'd not have stood a chance. He's kept them alive and he's kept his mouth shut.' Maman had her hand to her mouth. 'He couldn't have told you, Lise, he couldn't have. He'd given his word, and anyway you'd have only tried to stop him.' He turned back to Papa. 'Now, you may not know it where you've been hidden away, but there's a law hereabouts, laid down by our Boche friends, and it's this: anyone who's caught aiding or abetting the escape of fugitives will be shot. Jo's known that all the time he's been doing it. Every day of his life your son could have been taken out and shot.'

As Jo listened he was suddenly terrified, retrospectively terrified. Of course he'd known it but he'd not thought about it, not properly. It had never sunk in until now. It was as if Grandpère had been talking about someone else. There had been no real intention on his part. Things had just happened. When Grandpère had finished he looked at Papa. He was leaning forward, his head in his hands.

'Jo,' he said, 'what have I done to you? What've I said?'

'Nothing that can't be undone,' said Grandpère. 'Nothing that can't be unsaid. On your feet the two of you,' and he drew them together.

After they hugged, Papa held Jo by the shoulders, and smiled through his tears. 'You're taller than me,' he said, and he turned away. 'The children,' he went on. 'They're still up there then, up in the cave?'

'Still up there,' said Grandpère, and he told him all about Benjamin and Widow Horcada, and how they were waiting for the right moment to take the children over the mountains.

Papa walked to the mantlepiece and leant on it for a moment. Then he turned round. 'You're crazy, crazy,' he said. 'At any moment a patrol could stumble across that cave. What have you been waiting for – a miracle? For the war to end? For the Boche to fall asleep?'

'I told you,' said Grandpère, 'there's patrols out everywhere. Benjamin's seen them. I've seen them, and besides some of the children have been too weak to move.'

'Weak or not,' said Papa vehemently, 'they've got to go. If necessary they'll have to be carried, but they've got to go.'

'Just tell us how,' said Grandpère. 'You tell us how to do it and we'll do it. Don't you think we haven't thought about it?' Papa said nothing.

'Maybe,' said Maman quietly, 'maybe the children could pretend to be someone they weren't.'

'What do you mean?' Grandpère said.

'I don't know,' she said, 'I was just thinking aloud really. But I remember when I was little I was told some story about a one-eyed giant, and there were all these men in a cave and a giant was waiting outside to kill them as they came out, and there were some sheep sheltering inside the cave with them.'

'I know it, I remember it,' said Papa, and he went on. 'When the sheep come out of the cave they're all clinging on underneath and he doesn't see them. You're not suggesting...'

'No, of course I'm not,' said Maman, 'but sheep need shepherds don't they? It's been a warm spring. There'll be plenty of grass by now on the high pastures. By my reckoning there must be two thousand sheep in the village, a hundred cows or more, fifty horses maybe, and your pigs too, Grandpère. When the time's right, and after all we can choose when the time's right, they'll all be moving up into the mountains for the summer won't they? No one will notice a few more children shepherding them will they? And once you get up to the hut, well, it's like you always say, Grandpère, you're so close to Spain up there you could almost spit into it.'

They all looked at her.

'Just an idea,' she said.

CHAPTER 8

IT WAS STRANGE SEEING WIDOW HORCADA SITTING in their kitchen with Grandpère fussing around her. She and Maman were polite to each other but no more than that. She listened intently as Papa told her the plan. When it was over she sat back in her chair and wrinkled her nose. 'I don't know,' she said. 'I don't know. It seems to me the more people you tell the greater the risk that someone will talk, and you want to tell everyone.'

'But don't you see, Alice,' said Grandpère, 'everyone has to know, we need them to know, else they won't all come to the concert will they? And how else are we going to find enough clothes for the children, eh? Then we've got to find a place for them to sleep the night before and a family to look after them on the way up to the hut; and they've all got to act like they know the children. It just won't work unless everyone knows.'

'I know all that,' said the Widow. 'But can they all be trusted? Can you be sure of them, of every one of them? Madame Soulet? Armand Jollet?' No one answered. She went on. 'All you need is one of them to take fright, and after all, they'll know what'll happen to them if they're caught.'

'You knew,' said Maman quickly, 'and so did Jo and so did Grandpère. It didn't stop any of you doing what was right, did it?' The Widow looked at her sharply. 'No one's going to give them away,' Maman went on, 'because if they did they'd know it wouldn't be just the children in the cave who would suffer, it would be all of us – the whole of the village, everyone they've grown up with, all of us.'

'That's the beauty of it, Alice,' said Grandpère. 'Don't you see? We're all in it together, sink or swim. That's why everyone has to be part of it; and they'll want to be too when they hear about the children. There's some good folk in this village and they'll bring the others along with them.'

'They'll be frightened,' said Maman, 'like I was when Grandpère told me all about Jo and you and

those children up in the cave; and I'll tell you something else, I'm still frightened, but I know it has to be
done and so will they. They'll do it, you'll see.'

Widow Horcada smiled at Maman and chuckled.
'You've got some spirit in you, girl,' she said, 'more
than you ever let on, eh?' Jo had never heard his
mother so forthright, so determined.

'Well,' Papa said. 'Do we do it or don't we? We can't
stay talking about it for ever.'

The Widow Horcada looked at him steadily and
took a deep breath. 'We do it,' she said, 'and may God
help us.'

'Amen,' said Grandpère.

They spent the next hour or so compiling a list of
names. 'We've got to see every single one of them,' said
Papa. 'Monsieur Sarthol first, then Father Lasalle. If he
won't help us out with the concert, then we'll have to
call it off anyway; and then Monsieur Audap to see if
he'll let the children off school on Monday. We need
the children, more than anyone we need the children,
all of them.'

Father Lasalle announced the concert during Mass.
Everyone had been told about it by now and was
expecting it, except for the soldiers of course. Looking
directly at Lieutenant Weissmann and the dozen or so

soldiers sitting with him Father Lasalle spoke with his usual intoning drone but also with the authority of a man who was used to commanding attention. 'For three months every summer,' he said, 'our small community loses many of its men folk. As we all know, on Monday next begins the great exodus, the transhumance, the beginning of months of solitude and hard work. In Lescun it has always been thus. Now I have lived here amongst you for most of my life, long enough to know that some of these men might want to spend their last evening in the café, and that is something I would not wish to deny them even if I could. So by all means go to the café; but I want everyone, and I do mean everyone, to come here to the church afterwards.' Jo was looking along the pew towards the soldiers; he wanted to watch their faces for any flicker of disbelief. The Corporal leaned forward and winked at him and Jo looked away quickly.

'Vanity, vanity saith the preacher, all is vanity,' said Father Lasalle smiling broadly and putting his hand on his heart, 'and I confess freely to a great vanity. As you know, for many long hours I sit alone at the organ here in the church and I practise. I have been practising some of the greatest organ music ever written and it was written by a German too, one Johann Sebastian Bach. But for a musician practise is not enough. I must perform. My music must be heard. From time to time in the past I have given recitals and so tonight, to mark the eve of the transhumance I will be giving you one of my short concerts, and I want all of you here, a gathering of the entire community, every man, woman and child. No child is ever too young for Bach.' He leaned forward over the pulpit, his eyes raking the pews, his finger pointing. 'And you can be sure I shall know if you're not here.' There was some laughter at that. And then he spoke directly to Lieutenant Weissmann. 'The music, as I have said, will be German, Lieutenant. I know how fond you are of Bach and since it was written to glorify the God of both our peoples, you and your men will be most welcome. Catholic and Protestant, all will be welcome. Indeed, Lieutenant, I will be most disappointed if the entire German garrison is not here. Can I count on you, Lieutenant?' The Lieutenant nodded, smiling. 'That is kind of you, Lieutenant. I shall reserve seats for you. The concert will begin at eight o'clock and so it should be over well before curfew.' It was a masterly performance.

Father Lasalle's concerts were rarely well attended. That evening though the church was as full as Jo had ever seen it. But by five to eight the German soldiers had still not arrived. Jo sat next to Maman, her hand squeezing his. He squeezed back to reassure and be reassured. They would come, they had to come. Christine sat on the other side of her, thumb in her mouth, her legs swinging. The church was silent with expectation, not a murmur, not a cough. Jo turned and craned his neck. Still nothing. Maman pulled on his hand and he turned back again. The bells groaned in the tower and struck eight o'clock. Father Lasalle emerged from the vestry and looked at the empty pews where the soldiers should have been. He seemed uncertain what to do. At that moment the Lieutenant strode in, cap under his arm, the soldiers trooping in behind him. The sigh of relief was almost audible. Jo counted them in as Father Lasalle took his seat at the organ. Twenty-two. They were all there. Last to take their seats were the Mayor and Hubert. As they sat down in front of Jo he heard the doors close behind him.

The first piping notes sounded out through the church. Jo shivered, whether through pleasure or relief he did not know. From where he sat he could just see Father Lasalle's head rocking back and forth and the back of his heels stepping neatly across the foot pedals. Even the smallest children, Christine amongst them, were immediately absorbed in the music. Hubert was lost in it, his mouth open, his head nodding, but Jo found he could not keep his eye off the clock. He knew they needed at least an hour to be sure, an hour without soldiers in the streets, a clear hour to bring the children down from the cave and to hide them away in their allotted houses. Jo ventured a look at the Corporal. He was gazing up at the roof and his fingers were tapping out the rhythm on his knees.

At long last nine o'clock struck in horrible disharmony with the organ. Father Lasalle played on. There was a certain amount of shuffling and coughing now as people became more uncomfortable and the music too repetitive to hold their attention. Jo glanced across at Lieutenant Weissmann who was looking at his watch and whispering to the Corporal beside him. The Corporal shrugged his shoulders and smiled and then took out his handkerchief and blew his nose noisily. 'Keep going, Father,' Jo said to himself. 'Keep going, keep going.'

Hubert was fidgetting now and looking around the church through his binoculars until his father put a firm hand on his wrist and pulled his arm downwards. Hubert was not so easily deterred. Much to everyone's amusement he trained his binoculars on Father Lasalle and then on each of the soldiers in turn.

It was not far short of half past nine when the music built to a final crescendo leaving the church filled with a throbbing silence. The Mayor and Hubert led the enthusiastic applause and Father Lasalle came out to take his bows. He held up his hands and shrugged his shoulders. 'I'm afraid it lasted a little longer than I expected,' he said. 'Good night and God bless you.' Lieutenant Weissmann shook his hand and then came over to talk to the Mayor who nodded and turned to the audience. 'Ladies and gentlemen,' he announced. 'The Lieutenant has asked me to say that curfew is extended by half an hour tonight to allow us to get home at our ease. He asks us all to be home by ten o'clock.'

Jo danced his way through the crowd outside the porch and ran all the way home. He found Papa and Grandpère sitting at the kitchen table. Grandpère was pouring wine. 'Are they here?' he said.

'Up in the hayloft,' said Grandpère, 'all three of them.'

'Did you get them all?' said Jo.

'All of them,' said Papa, 'and they're all where they should be. We did it in under the hour.'

Jo climbed the ladder at the back of the barn and pushed open the loft door. 'Jo?' It was Benjamin's voice whispering out of the darkness. 'Is that you, Jo?'

'It's me,' he said, and he hauled himself up into the loft.

'Léah's fast asleep,' said Benjamin, and in the

darkness Jo could just make her out curled up tight against him, an arm thrown around his knee.

'I'm not.' It was Michael crawling towards them through the hay. 'Here,' he said. 'I brought you this.' He was trying to thrust something into Jo's hand. 'It's something you always wanted,' he said. 'Something you could never win. Squeeze it,' he said, 'and it'll bring you luck.' It was a chess piece, a white queen.

'I've told him, Jo,' said Benjamin. 'I've told him that for tomorrow he's your brother. And do you know what he told me, this horrible boy, he said if you were his brother he'd have taught you to play chess a lot better than you do.'

And then Jo saw Benjamin's face silhouetted for a moment against the window behind him. 'You cut your beard off,' said Jo.

'Your father's orders.' Benjamin stroked his chin. 'If you want to be taken for a native, he said, then you've got to look like one. It seems there's not many people round here with a red beard, so off it had to come. I feel a bit naked without it, a bit cold too. Still, it'll grow again. It had better do, hadn't it, or Anya won't recognise me when she sees me.'

'You're staying behind then,' said Jo.

'Yes,' said Benjamin. 'I'll see them safely over the border and then I'll come back.' He put his arm around him. 'Jo,' he said, 'I feel surer than ever that somehow Anya will find her way here. You remember what I said to you a while back when I hurt my ankle, when the snows came and it all looked hopeless? You remember what I said? I said "Wait and pray". Well we waited and we prayed and here we are. This time tomorrow, God willing, the children will be in Spain and they'll be safe at last. So I shall wait up in the cave for Anya, and I shall pray.'

When Jo went down to the kitchen they were all there and Papa was crouching down in front of Christine and holding her hands. There was an edge of impatience in his voice. 'Forget about the donkey, Christine, just remember – stay with Jo. You clap your hands when he does, and you chase the sheep like Rouf does, and if anyone asks you've got a big sister called Léah and a big brother called Michael. Do you understand now?'

'But I haven't got a big sister,' she said, 'and my big brother's called Jo.'

Papa gave up and Maman took his place. 'It's pretend, Christine,' she said. 'Just for tomorrow you've got a pretend sister and she's called Léah and you've got a pretend brother and he's called Michael and you've got to look after them, no squabbling.'

'But can I ride the donkey?' she said and everyone had to laugh.

When she'd gone up to bed Papa stretched out in his chair and Grandpère lit his last cigarette of the day – he always had a 'last one', usually several of them, before he went to bed. 'Some people,' he said, 'are so predictable. You know what Armand Jollet said when I told him? He said he ought to be compensated – compensated! You know what he said? He said, "If I go with you I'll have to close up the shop for a whole day and that'll cost me", and his chins shook like an agitated turkey. You should've seen him.'

'Money,' said Maman, 'it's all that man ever thinks of.'

'I've never really talked much to the schoolmaster, that Monsieur Audap,' said Papa. 'Always thought he was a strange fish. But he's not. He's a fine man. When I told him all about it and asked him about giving the children a day off school, he thought for a moment and I was sure he was going to refuse. He always looks such a miserable old so-and-so. Do you know what he said, Jo? He said the children would likely learn more in that one day than he could teach them in a lifetime. "Nothing's important unless it stays with you," that's what he said; "and no matter what happens, none of us," he said, "none of us is ever likely to forget tomorrow".'

Jo did not even try to sleep that night, he knew it

would be pointless. His mind went over the plan again and again. He tried to visualise it as the soldiers would see it. Would it all look normal to them? Would they notice all the extra children in amongst the animals? Would they catch a glimpse of Benjamin's face and know him for a stranger? He could almost convince himself that it was going to work, that the Germans would see only what they were supposed to see: but as the night wore on a terrible doubt kept recurring. It was something the Corporal had told him a long time ago. He'd come from a village in the mountains, in Bavaria, 'just like Lescun,' he'd said. Well, Jo thought, if it was a lot like Lescun then he'd know that you don't need dozens and dozens of children to drive the animals, he'd know you can do the job with a few men and a couple of dogs and he'd know too that the flocks and herds were moved out separately and not in one great, chaotic bunch. The more Jo saw it through the Corporal's eyes the more he worried, and by dawn a multitude of nagging doubts had eclipsed his hopes. He faced the day ahead with a deep dread welling inside him.

At breakfast he recognised the same anxiety in Maman's eyes. Papa and Grandpère were still arguing on and on about who would be best to stay with the children in the hut and guide them over the mountains. Grandpère said that he was fitter, that Papa's coughing could give them away. Papa said he was younger and that anyway he knew the mountains better. At one point they were going to do it together, but Maman would have none of that. She said it was silly for two of them to take the risk of getting caught. In the end it was Papa who had his way.

Léah and Michael looked awkward in their country clothes. They ate ravenously and in silence. Christine just stared at them and refused to eat her breakfast. 'Time to go, I think,' said Papa. Benjamin finished his coffee and stood up.

'Monsieur, Madame,' he said, 'I hardly know you, but before we leave I want to thank you and through you all the people of this village for what you have done and what you are about to do. What has happened here in this little place, whether it succeeds or whether it fails, is evidence enough, if any were needed, that no one will ever suppress the power for good, for compassion in the hearts of men and women. I have one regret though, that my little Anya is not yet here. But when she comes I shall tell her, I shall tell her often so that she can tell her children. Such things should not be forgotten. And now if you will allow me I will say a prayer. It is the last prayer we Jews say before we leave the Synagogue.' He closed his eyes.

'And the Lord shall be king over all the earth. In that day shall the Lord be one and His name be one.'

Rouf lay stretched out like a carpet by the stove with Léah crouched beside him stroking the top of his head. She leaned over and kissed him.

'Jo,' said Papa. 'You'd better wake that dog up. We can't move those sheep without him.' Jo whistled and Rouf woke, a look of resignation on his face. He yawned noisily and Léah laughed and sat back on her haunches as he stretched, shook himself awake, and then led them outdoors into the yard.

The streets were already full of sheep noise, a cacophony of bells and bleating and, claiming a bass line in the raucous choir, the cows bellowed and the donkeys brayed. The first flock came past them, Laurent driving them with his stick. He was leading a heavily laden donkey that stepped daintily over the cobbles. He winked at Jo as he passed and grinned. He was enjoying every minute of it. He had two of the cave children with him. They looked for all the world just like the village children around them. Like them they carried switches and sticks, like them they whistled and shouted and clapped. Two more flocks and a herd of cows came by, and Jo counted at least another five children from the cave.

Now it was their turn. Hubert was sitting on the

wall laughing and pointing as they gathered up the sheep in the yard. Jo shouted to him to open the gate and he began to flap his arms and whistle. Michael followed his example at once with uninhibited enthusiasm. When Benjamin too turned shepherd Léah seemed to warm to the idea and joined in as well. As he left the yard Jo turned and waved to Grandpère and Papa – they'd be coming on behind with the pigs and the donkey.

By the time they reached the Square Jo saw that the flocks had bunched together and every street leading into it was thick with sheep and cattle. The noise was deafening, an incessant chorus of animals punctuated with whooping and whistling and barking. Jo saw a sheep burst through the front door of Monsieur Sarthol's house, a dog went in after it. Jo never saw what happened for his eye was taken by something far more worrying. Three soldiers, one of them the Corporal, were standing on top of the wall by the war memorial and watching everything that passed through the Square below them. Jo looked away quickly and whooped even louder at the sheep. A cow was rubbing itself against the corner of the café and the soldiers were laughing. Benjamin was keeping his head down as Papa had suggested he should, but to Jo his shepherding looked somehow forced and stiff. And then he felt Léah clutching his arm. She had seen the soldiers and was looking up at them, her eyes wide with terror. The Corporal was looking right at her and the sheep would not move on. There was nothing Jo could do. There were sheep behind him, sheep in front of him, sheep all about him. The Corporal had let himself down off the wall and was scrutinising them closely. He had noticed something – Jo was sure of it.

Why Hubert chose that moment to perform Jo never knew but he pushed his way through the sheep and began to leap up and down like a wild thing; and then raising his arms in the air he growled at the sheep like a bear. The Corporal pointed and laughed and the other soldiers laughed with him. Hubert saw it and performed his bear act again, but with redoubled vigour. All around him the sheep panicked. They pushed and shoved and jumped over each other and at last the great flock began to move again up past the baker's shop. Jo slipped around the back of Léah, ostensibly to chase a sheep, but this way he'd be between her and the soldiers so that she could not see them and they could not see her. He dared not venture another look at the soldiers until they'd left the Square behind them. When he did turn round the Corporal was looking straight at him. Jo turned away quickly and played shepherd again.

So the chaotic cavalcade wound its way slowly out of the village and up towards the hills beyond. They could see the circle of mountains ahead of them. All around him Jo could see and feel the exhilaration and relief. The ruse had surely worked. The cave children had passed undetected under the nose of the Germans. The worst must be over. Even Rouf seemed to sense the triumph. He was chasing his tail and he only did that these days when he was high with happiness. But Jo could not share in the general elation. He could think only of the patrols they might meet before they reached the high pastures and the hut; but worse he could not get out of his head that the Corporal had guessed what they were up to. There had been a look in his eye – he was certain of it – a knowing look. 'We must make it look like a fête, a holiday,' Papa had said. 'We don't hurry it, we enjoy it.' And so they did. They reached the plateau by lunchtime. They picnicked by the stream and the animals browsed hungrily in the lush grass. They did not wander far because they did not need to.

It was proving almost impossible to keep the cave children away from each other. Benjamin spent his time persuading them to stay with their newly adopted families, but in spite of all he could do they seemed always to gravitate to each other again. It wasn't that the language was a barrier between them and the village children – after all some of the cave children were French – but there seemed to be an instinctive reserve that kept them apart.

It was only when Hubert appeared lumbering across thestream, four children clinging to his back, that they all found a mutual source of fun that brought cave children and village children together. Hubert, the great giant, had to be hauled down and held down and it took almost all of them to do it. In the pile of children on top of him they were all allies in the one cause. Michael and Laurent clung to the same leg and were shaken off. They rolled away together giggling before returning once more to the fray.

The afternoon climb was slow. It was steep now, up along narrow, tortuous tracks, where the sheep could only move in single file. The pigs hated climbing and were forever trying to wander off, and the cows too had had enough of it now. For many of the children the adventure had lost its early magic. Their legs ached, their feet hurt, and many of them had to ride. Every donkey now – every horse – was carrying at least one child. Christine insisted on sharing a donkey with Léah. Michael's leg had lasted well until he stumbled and fell. He limped on for a bit until Hubert noticed him. He led Michael to a rock and crouched down in front of it.

Michael climbed on and rode Hubert all the way up.

And so they came at long last to the high pastures, the horses first, then the sheep, the cows and last of all the reluctant pigs; and in amongst them all the hundred or so men, women and children who had brought them there. They lay down, man and beast, side by side, in silent exhaustion. They drank from the spring by the hut or from the stream that flowed from it. Michael and Jo cupped their hands in the spring and drank until they could drink no more. When Jo looked up the cave children were already being led towards the hut. 'Come on,' said Jo and they stood up.

'Is that Spain over there?' said Michael looking up at the peaks.

'That's Spain,' said Jo. They parted at the door of the hut.

'Don't lose my queen will you?' said Michael, and he went into the hut with the others.

When Jo turned round Benjamin was standing in front of him, Léah at his side. 'I'll be seeing you later then, Jo,' he said. Léah reached up and kissed him on the cheek. And then she was gone. He heard Papa's voice from inside the hut. 'Is that all of them? Have you counted them in?'

'That's all of them,' said Benjamin. 'All we've got to do now is wait until dark.'

Papa emerged from the hut and closed the door. 'You'd better get back down the mountain,' he said, and then his mouth fell open. He was looking over Jo's shoulder. Jo turned. Coming out of the trees were three soldiers. Everyone had seen them now. No one moved. No one said a word. There was no doubt about it, the one in front was the Corporal.

CHAPTER 9

THE CORPORAL WAS OUT OF BREATH. 'A HARD climb for an old man,' he said. 'You bring the pigs too?'

'We fatten them up on the whey,' said Papa. 'Waste not, want not.'

'Of course,' said the Corporal and he looked about him. 'Mountains,' he said. 'The transhumance. It must be the same the world over I expect; but back at home we have only the cows and horses. The horses, they are like yours except they have flaxen manes and tails – Haflingers we call them. But just like you do we take them all up to the high pastures in the summer; except of course we do not all go together.'

Papa was quick to explain – too quick, Jo thought. 'The shepherds will part them up this evening,' he said, 'and they'll take them off to their own mountainside. Every shepherd has his own mountainside.'

The Corporal nodded. 'Of course,' he said. 'Of course. Back at home,' he went on and he was looking straight at the hut as he spoke, 'back at home it is just the men who drive the animals, and their dogs of course. No women, no children. You must have almost the whole village up here.'

Hubert came running across to the Corporal and looked at him through his binoculars from a metre away. The Corporal smiled and winked into the binoculars. 'Hello Hubert,' he said, but Jo could see he was still interested in the hut. 'And you pass the whole summer alone up here?'

Papa leaned back against the door of the hut. 'That's right,' he said.

'Do you mind if we fill our water bottles?' the Corporal asked.

'Go ahead,' said Papa.

'Hans,' said the Corporal, holding out his water bottle and pointing to the spring. He turned back to Papa. 'So you have to do all the work yourself, the milking, the shepherding, the cheesemaking.'

'Everything,' said Papa watching the soldier as he crouched beside the spring. 'I take the donkey down to the village once a week with the cheeses, pick up supplies and I'm back here in time to milk them in the evening.'

A shutter squeaked and banged open in the wind. The soldier at the spring looked up once and then looked again, his eyes squinting. He screwed the top on the water bottle and stood up, his eyes still on the shutter that swung back and forth now on its hinges. He began to walk towards it. No one moved a muscle.

'That must be hard work,' said the Corporal, but Papa was not listening. His face was frozen. Jo could feel the queen in his pocket and squeezed it until his eyes watered. He looked up at the Corporal and their eyes met. In that moment the Corporal knew and understood. Jo was sure of it.

'Hans,' the Corporal shouted. Hans hesitated looking from the window to the Corporal and back again. 'Hans,' said the Corporal, more quietly this time. '*Kommen sie zurück. Nichts da.*' The soldier shrugged his shoulders and came back. The Corporal turned to Papa. 'You should get that mended,' he said. 'If you do not, it will blow off in the first storm.' And then he spoke to everyone. 'Lieutenant Weissmann has sent me out to escort you all back,' he said. 'We shall need to start down now I think. I am sure you know that you must be back inside your homes before curfew.'

No one needed to be asked twice. Families gathered

together briefly to say goodbye to their men and then they followed the soldiers past the piggery and the donkey shelter and made their way down towards the tree line. The last Jo saw of Papa he was standing at the door of the hut, the other shepherds around him. Jo lifted his hand to wave and then a rock was between them and he could see them no more.

With Christine on his shoulders Hubert walked beside Jo all the way down the mountain. Hardly anyone spoke. The soldiers walked on ahead of them, stopping every now and then to let them catch up. Once at the river everyone stopped to rest and Jo looked around for the Corporal. He was sitting on his own, his back to everyone, tugging at the grass beside him. Hubert went to sit beside him and showed him how he could make rude noises by blowing the grass through his thumbs. The Corporal seemed preoccupied and disinterested; and after a few moments Hubert got up and moved away to blow on his grass alone. Jo wanted to go right up to the Corporal there and then to thank him. He wanted to tell everyone what the Corporal had done. If only they knew what he knew they would be carrying him shoulder high into the village. As it was, when they got back home they all vanished into their houses bursting with the news of their success. Jo could hear it now, the same story in every house, about how the children would be over the border tonight and away, and about how they'd had a bit of luck up by the hut, but that otherwise it had all gone according to plan. And sure enough that was precisely the story Grandpère told Maman as soon as they got in.

'One look through that window,' said Grandpère, 'and that would've been that. Makes me sick just to think about It. If the Corporal hadn't picked that moment to call the soldier away then God only knows what would have happened.'

'Perhaps it was the prayer Benjamin said this morning,' said Maman.

'Maybe,' said Grandpère. Jo thought then of speaking up. He had to force himself not to. What the Corporal had done he'd done for him. It was personal and it was private and he could tell no one, not ever.

The village always seemed an empty echoing place that first morning after the transhumance, and sad too; but the mood when Jo reached school that morning was jubilant. Everyone had been told time and again never to talk about the escape, never ever to mention it; but they still gathered in conspiratorial huddles and relived their exploits. Jo was uneasy though, and he had good cause. From dawn they'd been expecting word that the children had crossed safely over into

Spain. It had all been arranged. The Widow Horcada was going to let them know just as soon as Benjamin got back. But there had been no word. 'No news is good news,' Grandpère kept saying – rather too often Jo thought.

All through first lesson that morning Jo looked out of the window and tried to convince himself that nothing could have gone wrong. After all, what could go wrong between the hut and the border? 'So close you could spit into Spain,' that's what Grandpère alwayssaid. Jo squeezed the queen in his pocket and closed his eyes for a moment. He tried to pray but he couldn't. He tried to obliterate his worst fears, but he could not. The night had been pitch black and perfect. Papa was there to guide them over. They couldn't have got lost. They'd go the silent way, walking on the grass not across the scree. There'd be someone waiting for them on the other side to take the children on into Spain. Benjamin and Papa would be back in the hut by midnight at the latest – Papa had said as much. They were going to rest for an hour or two before the descent, and Papa was going to bring Benjamin down as far as the river and let him go on back to Widow Horcada's house alone. Nothing could have gone wrong. No news was good news. Please God.

'Jo?' Monsieur Audap was coming towards his

desk. 'I don't think you've been entirely with us this morning, Jo. If you've seen the view out of that window once you've seen it a thousand times. Now, whilst I appreciate you are not a natural mathematician...' The door burst open and Hubert was standing there, his mouth open, straining to make intelligible words out of his grunting. He was beckoning frantically. 'Stay where you are all of you,' said Monsieur Audap. 'I'll be back in a minute.' But Jo was out of the door even before he was. Hubert took his arm and ran with him down towards the Square. By the time they reached it Jo expected to find it full of the cave children, but it was empty. There were heads at every window and people standing in the street craning to look. Jo was about to run on but a hand held him back firmly. Monsieur Audap was at his side and the school children had filled the street behind him. Madame Soulet came out of her shop wiping her hands on her apron and Jo saw her look up the street and then rush back inside and shut the door. The next moment her face appeared pale in the window, and now Jo could see what she had seen.

There was a soldier in front and one on either side, and there was someone else between them but Jo still could not make out who it was. And then he knew who it was and his heart turned cold. It looked like one person at first, but it was two. Benjamin was carrying Léah, her arms around his neck, her head buried in his shoulder. He stopped now and put her down. He crouched down and straightened her coat, talking to her all the while. Then he took her hand and they walked slowly into the Square, which was filling now with silent people. From behind Jo came the sound of running boots. Lieutenant Weissmann, the Corporal and a dozen soldiers pushed their way through the school children and into the Square. Soldiers fanned out all over the Square driving the crowd back. One of the soldiers saluted as Lieutenant Weissmann came up. Jo could understand nothing of what was being said but he heard one word repeated over and over again, '*Juden*'. The Lieutenant walked across to Benjamin and looked at him and then down at Léah. 'You are Jews?' he asked.

Benjamin smiled and nodded. 'We are,' he said. 'May we sit down please? The little girl is very tired and so am I.' The Corporal pulled out two chairs from outside the café and they sat down side by side still holding hands.

Lieutenant Weissmann looked around him. 'Is Monsieur Sarthol here?' he said. Monsieur Sarthol stepped out of the crowd. 'Monsieur Sarthol,' said the Lieutenant, 'I must get these two down to the station at once. They'll never get there on foot. My horse is lame, so I will need a horse, a donkey, whatever you can find.'

Monsieur Sarthol nodded. 'You heard what the Lieutenant said,' he said. 'He needs a donkey or a horse.' No one spoke. 'For God's sake, do you want them to have to walk?'

'They can have mine,' said Monsieur Audap, and then he turned to Jo. 'Fetch her, Jo, will you?' he said quietly. 'You know where to find her saddle.' Jo hesitated. 'Fetch her,' said Monsieur Audap, an edge to his voice.

Laurent went with him. 'What happened?' he said as they ran up the hill. 'What went wrong?'

'I don't know,' said Jo. 'I don't know.' It was all he could do to hold back his tears.

They found Monsieur Audap's mare and saddled her up together. Laurent held her mane as Jo slipped the bridle over her ears.

'What'll they do with them?' said Laurent.

'One of those camps,' said Jo.

The crowd parted as they led the horse into the Square. Benjamin was talking urgently to Léah, smoothing her hair. They looked up and saw Jo coming towards them. Neither showed any flicker of recognition. Jo held the horse as Benjamin mounted from a chair. The Corporal handed Léah up to him and she sat clutching the mane, Benjamin's arm around her.

'You'll be escorted to the train by the Corporal,' said the Lieutenant.

'And after that?' said Benjamin.

'That is not my concern,' said the Lieutenant and he stepped aside.

A soldier took the reins from Jo. Jo looked up at Benjamin who held out his hand. *'Dziękuję,'* he said. Jo took his hand. *'Dziękuję,'* Benjamin said again. For a moment Léah's eyes met Jo's and held them.

The Lieutenant was frowning at him. 'Do you know them?' he said. Jo shook his head.

'Of course not,' said Benjamin. 'We know no one here and no one knows us. The boy brought me a horse and I simply said thank you. Is it not permitted for a Jew even to say thank you?'

Jo watched them being led away, the horse's hooves slipping on the cobbles as she was led across the Square, down the hill and out of sight. Monsieur Audap tried to gather the children together and take them back to school; but many, like Jo, drifted away homewards. As he walked home through the empty streets he gleaned from the squeeze of Benjamin's hand, from the single word Benjamin had been able to say to him, all that he had wanted to say and was not able to say without betraying him.

The news had reached home before him. Papa was sitting hunched over the table, head in his hands. He looked up as Jo came in, his eyes full of tears. 'You mustn't go blaming yourself,' said Maman. She prised his hands away from his face and kissed them. 'We all did what we could, everyone did.'

'Did we?' said Grandpère fiercely. 'I was in the Square just now. There were over a hundred of us and just twenty-two of them – and we just stood and watched them take them away.' He looked away to hide his face.

'What happened, Papa?' said Jo. 'The children, did they get away?'

'Oh yes,' said Papa, 'we got them away just like we planned. Like clockwork it was. We were up at the border before midnight. Only one thing went wrong. The little girl.'

'Léah,' said Grandpère.

'She wouldn't leave him,' Papa went on. 'I tell you, Jo, I've never seen anything like it. The strength of the girl. There wasn't much of her but she clung to Benjamin like she would drown if she let go. So we had to bring her back with us to the hut – there was nothing else we could do. Even then we weren't too unhappy. We had a glass together in the hut, Benjamin and me, to celebrate it was, before we came down. The little girl was tired of course, so I sat her on the donkey and we set off.' He drank down his glass and wiped his mouth with the back of his hand. 'But then it happened. I thought it was a boar. There was a sort of snorting, growling. You couldn't see anything, not at first. It's funny though, Benjamin seemed to know at once what it was, almost like he was expecting it. He shouted some sort of warning to the little girl. I don't know what he said, but I understood soon enough when that bear came lumbering out of the trees. He came right at us. Benjamin stood his ground and faced him, but the donkey took off, the little girl screaming loud enough to wake the dead. I was running like the donkey was. You don't stand and fight a bear; but when I turned round I saw Benjamin throwing stones at it and shouting at it and the bear was backing away. I couldn't believe it and then I remembered all about that bear cub you told me about, the one that Benjamin brought up, and I put two and two together; so I started throwing stones at him too. He was up on his hind legs and waving his paws like he was boxing and we were hitting him again and again and still he came on. Then it seemed like he'd had enough of it and he went down on all fours and just walked off. All the time we could hear the little girl crying and screaming somewhere behind us and the donkey braying down in the valley. I went after the donkey, Benjamin went after the little girl.' Papa shook his head. 'I should never have left him. I should never have left him. I was gone a few minutes. Took me a bit of time to calm the donkey down. I was leading him back up through the trees towards them. The little girl, she was still crying like she would never stop and he was trying to comfort her. Then suddenly there were torchlights and shouting and there were soldiers everywhere. And what did I do? I crouched there in the darkness like a frightened rabbit, that's what I did. And I stayed there until I was sure they had gone. What does that make me, eh? You've a coward for a father, Jo.'

Jo put out his hand to touch Papa's shoulder. 'He said "thank you",' said Jo. 'Benjamin, he said to thank you.' Papa looked away.

'Someone's got to go up there and tell Alice,' said Grandpère, 'and I don't know if I can, not on my own.'

'I'll come,' Maman said, standing up and wrapping her shawl about her. 'Jo, you can stay here and look after your sister.' She put her arms around Papa's neck and kissed him on the top of the head. 'You'd better get yourself back up the mountain, those sheep won't milk themselves.' She took Grandpère's arm. 'Come on,' she said. 'Let's get this over with.'

In the days that followed the exodus of the cave children an unseasonal fog settled over the village and it matched perfectly the mood of the place. Yet even when it cleared and they began to cut the hay the village seemed incapable of lifting itself out of its gloom, and that in spite of the news of the war. It was all good. France was being liberated from the north and from the south too. The end of the occupation could not be far off now, but few in Lescun could rejoice in it.

No one spoke to the German soldiers any more. When people saw them coming they turned their backs and walked away. The soldiers scarcely ever ventured into the café and if they did they were met with a hostile silence that soon drove them out. There was no more nostalgic talk of old battles, no more sweets for the children.

Jo did all he could to avoid the Corporal, not because he blamed him for what had happened to Benjamin or Léah – he knew that was none of the Corporal's doing – but because he had come at last to see him as a man in the uniform of the enemy, a good and kindly man Jo had no doubt of that, but nonetheless an enemy too. It was a confusion he did not wish to confront. Their eyes met several times across the street but they never spoke, not until the evening Jo ran into the church porch to escape a torrential downpour, his jacket over his head. When he pulled it off he saw the Corporal standing beside him in the shadows.

'Hello Jo,' he said. Jo made to move away. 'No one can see us, Jo.' The Corporal took off his cap and shook it. 'Hubert gave me back the binoculars.'

'I know,' Jo said.

'But the little cup he made, I shall keep it. I shall take it home when this is over, and it will not be long now I think. It will remind me of this place, of him, of you.'

'They were taken to one of those camps, weren't they?' said Jo. The Corporal said nothing.

'But why?' said Jo. 'What for? What did they do?'

The Corporal took a deep breath and let it out slowly. 'I have no answers, Jo,' he said. 'I know no answers, no reasons. I have thought much of that man and the little girl, and still I do not understand.'

'He was a friend of mine,' said Jo fiercely. 'They both were. He was hiding up in the mountains, and do you know why? He was waiting for his daughter to come so they could escape together into Spain. He wouldn't leave without her.'

'The little girl, she was his daughter?'

'That was Léah,' said Jo. 'His daughter's called Anya. He was so sure she would come, but she never did.' The Corporal put on his cap and made to move away. 'That day up at the hut,' Jo went on. 'You knew, didn't you?'

The Corporal nodded. 'I thought there was someone inside,' he said, 'someone or maybe something you did not want me to see.'

'There was,' said Jo. 'There were twelve Jewish children, and they escaped. All except Léah, they escaped.' And he did not try to disguise the triumph in his voice.

'Well, well,' said the Corporal. 'I suppose that's something. *Auf Wiedersehen* Jo.' And pulling up the collar of his coat he walked out into the rain.

They were carting in the hay a few days later when Jo thought he heard the sound of distant thunder. Maman brought the horse to a halt and Grandpère held up his hand. It wasn't thunder, it was drumming. It was Hubert drumming. Christine screamed at being left behind but Jo ran on ahead anyway. As he ran down through the streets he was aware there were others running with him, all around him now; and the drumming echoed off the walls of the houses so that it seemed as if Hubert must be beating a dozen drums. In the Square they were all hugging each other and crying. 'They've gone!' Jo heard. 'The Germans have gone!'

The bells were ringing and Monsieur Sarthol was

leaning out of the window of the Mairie and fumbling with a faded tricolour that would not run out on its pole, but when it did it was greeted with such a din of clapping and cheering that Jo couldn't hear what Laurent was shouting in his ear, not at first. 'Hubert!' he shouted. 'Look at Hubert!' Outside the café they were drinking straight from the bottles, arms around each other and dancing; and Hubert was standing by his drum and drinking wine as if it were water. He finished the bottle and raised his hands in the air, laughing till the tears ran down his face. When Jo saw him next he was dancing around the Square with Christine, it was a wild gallop more than a dance but Christine was loving it.

Monsieur Sarthol stood on the war memorial and tried to make a speech but no one would listen so he gave up and sang the Marseillaise instead, bottle in hand. By the end of it everyone was linking arms and singing with him. Then Father Lasalle was running in amongst them. 'Quick!' he shouted, tugging Monsieur Sarthol by the arm. 'Quick! It's Hubert, he's in the churchyard. I think he's gone mad. He's trying to push away one of the tombstones.' And Jo knew at once which tombstone.

He was there before anyone. The tombstone was ajar and Hubert was nowhere to be seen. He didn't need to look in to see if Grandpère's rifle was still there. It would be gone, he knew it. From the graveyard wall he could see Hubert springing down the hillside, the rifle held above his head; and on the winding track below the village the grey column of German soldiers led by Lieutenant Weissmann on his horse. 'Don't Hubert! Don't!' he called, and he saw Lieutenant Weissmann swivel in his saddle and look upwards. 'Don't shoot!' Jo cried. 'Don't shoot!' Hubert had stopped. He was aiming the rifle at the soldiers. Jo vaulted the wall and ran screaming down the hill waving his hands. He leapt the ditch and blundered through the hedges and all the while he called out, 'Hubert! Hubert! Don't! Don't!'

He never saw the shooting, he tripped over a root and was picking himself up when he heard it. There were just two shots. He looked where Hubert had been and could not see him.

Lieutenant Weissmann was running up the hill towards him, a pistol in his hand. Jo found Hubert lying on his back in the long grass, the rifle still grasped in his hand. His eyes were looking at the sun but not seeing. Jo looked at the blood on the grass by his shoe and thought of the bear lying stretched out on the chairs in the Square all those years before. The blood of a man was the same red as the blood of a bear.

A shadow came over him and he looked up. Lieutenant Weissmann was looking down at him. He crouched down beside Hubert and felt his neck. 'A pity,' he said and he stood up. 'I am sorry, very sorry.'

'He didn't mean it,' said Jo as the Lieutenant walked away; and then he was shouting after him. 'He didn't mean it! He didn't mean it...'

A few months later the war was over. The men from the prisoner-of-war camps came home, or most of them did. Everyone waited for some word of Benjamin and Léah, but there was no word; instead came the first dreadful rumours, rumours that there were some camps – concentration camps – where Jews and others had been systematically murdered. Even when there were pictures in the newspapers and reports on the wireless Widow Horcada refused to believe it. Jo clung to Benjamin's own maxim: 'Wait and pray,' he had said 'Wait and pray'; but often alone in the cold church he would cry into his hands, for he somehow knew that his prayers were too late.

Meanwhile Monsieur Audap had been making enquiries. It seemed that Benjamin and Léah had been taken first to Gurs concentration camp about thirty kilometres away. From there they had been sent on to Auschwitz. Auschwitz was a death camp, he said. There were only a few survivors, and Benjamin and Léah were not amongst them. Like millions of Jews they would not be coming home.

Grandpère broke the news to Widow Horcada and was a constant source of comfort through her dark and grieving days. It was to no one's great surprise when the two of them got married just before the winter snows set in. Grandpère moved out of the house 'to start all over again' as he put it, up at Widow Horcada's farm. He took the pigs with him and that pleased Papa who could never take to them.

Jo left school the next Summer and became a full-time shepherd. With only Rouf for company he took the sheep up to the mountains and lived in the hut as Papa and Grandpère had done before him. Rouf was all the company he needed or sought. He buried himself in his work – it was the only way to forget the gnawing pain inside him. But at nights asleep in his hut the faces of Hubert, Benjamin and Léah haunted his dreams.

One Sunday afternoon, with the cheesemaking done, Jo was resting on his bed with Rouf beside him. It was the dog who heard the voices first and lifted his head. Then Jo heard Papa coughing and Christine prattling on. They often came up on a Sunday for a picnic. Jo had to steel himself to be sociable. Papa would question him endlessly about the sheep and

Christine would want her ride on the donkey. He was surprised though when he heard Widow Horcada's voice too. He swung his legs off the bed as Grandpère put his head round the door.

'Not disturbing you are we?' he said.

Jo blinked in the bright sunlight and held his hand over his eyes so that he could see better. They were all there. Papa was helping Widow Horcada down from her horse and Maman had the picnic basket on her arm. Rouf was greeting Christine in his usual boisterous way, paws on her shoulders. She staggered back and sat down hard, Rouf on top of her. She laughed and everyone laughed.

'Well, Jo,' said Widow Horcada shaking out her skirts. 'Have you lost your tongue? Don't you know how to say hello to strangers?'

'Strangers?' said Jo.

And then he saw the girl. She was walking towards him. She had red hair that she pushed back out of her eyes and tucked behind her ears.

'I'm Anya,' she said.

EGMONT PRESS: ETHICAL PUBLISHING

Egmont Press is about turning writers into successful authors and children into passionate readers – producing books that enrich and entertain. As a responsible children's publisher, we go even further, considering the world in which our consumers are growing up.

Safety First
Naturally, all of our books meet legal safety requirements. But we go further than this; every book with play value is tested to the highest standards – if it fails, it's back to the drawing-board.

Made Fairly
We are working to ensure that the workers involved in our supply chain – the people that make our books – are treated with fairness and respect.

Responsible Forestry
We are committed to ensuring all our papers come from environmentally and socially responsible forest sources.

For more information, please visit our website at www.egmont.co.uk/ethical

Egmont is passionate about helping to preserve the world's remaining ancient forests. We only use paper from legal and sustainable forest sources, so we know where every single tree comes from that goes into every paper that makes up every book.

This book is made from paper certified by the Forestry Stewardship Council (FSC®), an organisation dedicated to promoting responsible management of forest resources. For more information on the FSC, please visit **www.fsc.org**. To learn more about Egmont's sustainable paper policy, please visit **www.egmont.co.uk/ethical**.